OPEN FOR BUSINESS

OPEN FOR BUSINESS

TALES OF OFFICE SEX

Edited by
Alison Tyler

CLEIS
PRESS

Published in the United States by Cleis Press Inc., P.O. Box 14697, San Francisco, California 94114.

Printed in the United States.
Cover design: Scott Idleman
Cover photograph: Betsie Van der Meer / Getty Images
Text design: Frank Wiedemann
Cleis Press logo art: Juana Alicia
First Edition.
10 9 8 7 6 5 4 3 2 1

"That Monday Morning Feeling" by Lisette Ashton originally appeared in *I Is for Indecent*, edited by Alison Tyler; "Headhunter" by CB Potts originally appeared in *Lipstick on Her Collar*, edited by Sacchi Green and Rakelle Valencia; "Late for Work" by Shelly Jansen originally appeared in *Penthouse Variations*; "Secretary's Day" by Rachel Kramer Bussel originally appeared in *Yes, Ma'am: Erotic Stories of Male Submission*, edited by Rachel Kramer Bussel; "Perks of the Job" by Kristina Wright originally appeared in *Naughty Spanking Stories from A to Z*, volume 2, edited by Rachel Kramer Bussel; "TGIF" by Saskia Walker originally appeared in *Hide and Seek*, edited by Alison Tyler and Rachel Kramer Bussel; "After Hours" by Marilyn Jaye Lewis originally appeared in *Naughty Spanking Stories from A to Z*, volume 2, edited by Rachel Kramer Bussel.

Work saves us from three great evils:
boredom, vice, and need.
—Voltaire

Dance like it hurts,
Love like you need money,
Work when people are watching.
—Scott Adams

I like work: it fascinates me.
I can sit and look at it for hours.
—Jerome K. Jerome

MEMO: While You Were Out
For: AUSTIN, KARA, FELICE, FRÉDÉRIQUE & SAM
From: ALISON

(X) Telephoned
( ) Returned Your Call
( ) Came to See You
( ) Please Call
( ) Will Call Again
(X) Urgent

Message:
Dedicated, with love, to all of the above.

XXX,
ALISON

Contents

ix   *Introduction*

1   *That Monday Morning Feeling* • LISETTE ASHTON
9   *This Call May Be Monitored For Quality Assurance* •
     XAVIER ACTON
14   *Sex, Lies, and Library Books* •
     DONNA GEORGE STOREY
24   *Taking Care of Business* • SOMMER MARSDEN
31   *How to Fuck Your Boss* • ELIZABETH YOUNG
35   *Headhunter* • CB POTTS
42   *Late for Work* • SHELLY JANSEN
52   *In the Empire of Lust* • MAXIM JAKUBOWSKI
58   *Casual Friday* • JOLENE HUI
66   *Strict Management* • T.C. CALLIGARI
74   *Lunch Meeting* • MARIE SUDAC
77   *Secretary's Day* • RACHEL KRAMER BUSSEL
90   *One Cubicle Over* • JEREMY EDWARDS
98   *Perks of the Job* • KRISTINA WRIGHT
108 *Lonely at the Top* • SAVANNAH STEPHENS SMITH
121 *On the 37th Floor* • TULSA BROWN
130 *Have a Nice Day* • MIKE KIMERA
139 *Page Ten of the Employee Handbook* • ALISON TYLER
144 *TGIF* • SASKIA WALKER
156 *After Hours* • MARILYN JAYE LEWIS
167 *Memorandum* • N.T. MORLEY
175 *Rat Race* • NIKKI MAGENNIS

177 *About the Authors*
184 *About the Editor*

| INTRODUCTION

We've all heard the saying, "All work and no play makes Jack a dull boy." Luckily for Jack as well as the rest of us, here are twenty-two short stories filled with the art of playing at work...or *fucking* at work. You see, Jack? Even the most mundane nine-to-five job can lend itself to a rowdy romp that's sure to leave people talking by the water coolers for years to come. Because here are *special* offices, offices where naughty secretaries are firmly spanked, where cold callers hook up with dominatrixes, where temps find the men of their dreams washing their windows, and where wantonly, willfully sleeping your way to the top is considered a good thing.

This anthology will take you through the whole work week, from the morning commute ("That Monday Morning Feeling" by Lisette Ashton) to the bliss of a Friday ("TGIF" by Saskia Walker), with a few after-hours parties (by Marilyn Jaye Lewis and Sommer Marsden) and a three-martini lunch or two thrown in.

XXX,
Alison Tyler

THAT MONDAY MORNING FEELING

Lisette Ashton

It was the only thing that made the start of the working week bearable.

Mandy stepped out of the shower, her skin jeweled with beads of water and her pussy bare and tingling after enduring the closest of close shaves. She toweled herself quickly dry, conscious that there would only be time for one more cup of coffee before she left for the office.

Short black skirt.

Patent-leather black heels.

Low-cut white blouse.

Decaf.

And then she was out of the house, slamming the door closed and stepping onto the bus with the flavor of coffee beans still warming her mouth. Her hair was tied neatly back—pony-tailed into a glossy length of raven tresses that fell between her shoulder blades. A small black purse completed the mono-chrome ensemble she always wore for the colorless experience of the office week. And Mandy savored the special thrill that came from being without bra or panties beneath her clothes on the Monday morning commute.

Not that being without underwear was the only thing that made the start of the working week bearable.

It was much more than that.

Standing room only on the bus meant she was jostled between an eclectic crowd of mature men in suits and yobbish youths in jeans and leathers. The scents of deodorant, aftershave, and sweat mingled like the headiest of erotic perfumes. Through the windows, the gray world outside was a drab and cheerless background to the journey. If not for the excitement of her adventure, Mandy would have thought the view bleak and depressing. At the first stop another queue of morning commuters climbed onto the bus. The crowded interior became more claustrophobic and cramped. Everyone shuffled closer together to make room for the newcomers.

Mandy pushed her rear against the groin of a thirty-something executive. She had noticed him standing behind her. His cheeks were dirtied by the sort of designer stubble that made her think of too much testosterone, men at the gym and rugged movie stars playing the roles of escaped convicts. With only a glance at his face, she knew that kissing him would leave her lips sore, scratched, and bruised and desperate for more. If they became lovers she imagined he would be hard, brutal, greedy, and demanding. His shoulders were broad inside his off-the-rail Armani clone. His vast physical presence towered over her as he clutched the safety strap descending from the bus's roof.

She squirmed her rear against him.

The thrust of his semisoft length pushed back.

Mandy shivered.

She knew she could have enjoyed a similar tactile thrill if she had been wearing panties beneath her skirt. Another layer of clothing would not have greatly hampered the sensation of the executive's concealed cock probing at her thinly veiled buttocks. But the decadence of being without underwear, and knowing that she was so close to sliding her bare sex against the stranger, was sufficient to make her temperature soar. Savoring the delicious frisson of his trousers gliding against her skirt, Mandy imagined she could hear the bristle of the fabrics as they slipped coarsely against each other. The grumble of the bus's engine was loud enough that she knew she couldn't really hear those sounds. There was a muted babble of conversation around her: loud enough to be deafening and low enough to be indecipherable. But, as the stranger's length thickened against her rear, she fancied herself aware of every minute detail.

She believed she could hear the sound of his suit scratching at her skirt. She believed she could smell the vital scent of his pre-come and the musky ripeness of her own, wet sex. Arousal knotted her stomach muscles. If she had glanced down at her chest, Mandy knew she would have seen the tips of her nipples jutting against the flimsy fabric of her blouse. But instead of looking down at herself, she kept her gaze fixed ahead as she subtly squirmed her backside against the executive.

He was fully hard.

The thrust of his erection pushed at her skirt. If not for the protective shield of his trousers, Mandy knew his throbbing cock could have slipped between her buttocks and pushed easily into her.

She rubbed more firmly against him, pretending she was moving with the sway of the bus, slyly shifting from side to side and writhing until she heard his soft, satisfied sigh.

The bus drew to a halt.

Without sparing a backward glance, Mandy elbowed

through the crowd of commuters and left the bus. She kept her gaze averted as the vehicle drove away—not caring if the executive was watching, not caring if he was intrigued, infatuated, or indifferent. It was enough to know that she had already made one man hard this morning. Her backside tingled pleasantly where his erection had pressed against her. Her arousal was a strong and heady constant.

With the tube train due in mere moments, she had to rush away from the bus stop, into the underground station, and down three long escalator flights for the next stage of her journey.

The platform wasn't busy.

The air inside the underground station was arid and tasted of rust. The electric train throbbed like a pulse of charged sexuality. Mandy took a seat in a comparatively empty carriage. The only other occupant was a student in torn jeans and a Green Day T-shirt. Mandy sat opposite him and stretched as though she were still sleepy from the early start to the day.

Her blouse pulled tight across her chest.

She didn't need to glance down to know her nipples were jutting obviously against the thin fabric. The pressure against them was already sending delicious thrills through her body. Her cheeks were rouged with the blush of sexual excitement.

The Green Day student grinned.

With the skill of a practiced tease, Mandy avoided making eye contact. She rubbed the palm of her left hand down her sparsely clothed body, gliding her spread fingers from her breast, over her hip, and down to her bare knee. It was an exaggerated gesture of faux innocence. Mandy savored the sensation of caressing herself. Her left nipple was instantly ablaze. Her thigh bristled from the contact. Her skin was alive with a welter of greedy responses—tormented by her touch—and she was eager to suffer more.

From the corner of her eye Mandy noticed the student had pushed a hand against his crotch. His face was a grimace. He licked his lips with an obvious and impotent hunger.

Eager to be more daring, determined to give him a good show, Mandy glanced down at herself and then stroked the stiff bud of flesh that pushed at the fabric of her blouse.

The sensation was sublime.

She caught the stiff nipple between her finger and thumb and squeezed it gently. A crackle of arousal jolted her frame. Although she had known the pleasure would be intense, she hadn't expected it to strike with such power and force.

She gasped. And then, as she moved her hand away, she glanced up and met the student's appreciative gaze. His eyes were wide. His fist was crushed into his lap. His jaw was clenched. He sat forward in his chair as though a more natural position was too uncomfortable to tolerate.

Feigning an embarrassed smile, Mandy stood up and walked past him.

"Sorry," she mumbled. "I hadn't noticed you sitting there."

While he was still fumbling to respond, trying to cover his lap with a notebook and mumbling something she didn't hear, the tube reached its station and Mandy hurried from the train to make her next stop on the underground.

Another tube.

A busier route.

The station on this platform was packed with commuters. Each passing train was filled to bursting with tightly compressed bodies. Mandy shivered excitedly at the thought of being crammed in among so many strangers. The eerily dry air of the underground stroked a languid caress against her bare sex. Every time a new train arrived at the platform, it brought a warm, rushing breeze that was like the kiss of a lover's lips. She crushed her thighs together as the pleasure churned her stomach and made her briefly dizzy.

When she had neared the front of the queue for the approaching train, a daring idea crossed her mind. The concept was so exciting, she was almost too thrilled to act on it.

Another train thundered to the platform.

The doors of the train hissed open, and she squeezed into the carriage, telling herself this was too great an opportunity to miss. She was standing with her back to the windows and the platform beyond. A substantial crowd remained, some of them glowering at the full train, most of them waiting with resigned patience, a few of them meeting Mandy's inquisitive gaze.

Mandy reached behind herself for the hem of her skirt and lifted it.

She continued to stare over her shoulder, watching for a response.

A dozen slack-jawed faces stared admiringly at the pert cheeks of her exposed backside. She could see eyes wide with appreciation and grins of raw, animal lust. If there had been the space to move aboard the train, she would have bent forward and given her admiring audience a full view of her bare sex. If it hadn't been so cramped inside the train, she would have bent forward and then stroked a finger between her labia so that all the waiting commuters could watch as she teased herself to an exhibitionist climax.

Then the train was speeding off.

Her audience disappeared as the train hurried into a tunnel.

And Mandy consoled herself with the knowledge that she had provided a brief flash of excitement to a good many morning travelers.

Alighting at the next stop, following the escalator up three flights and drinking in the cool morning air, she checked her wristwatch before walking across the road to the office building.

The lift was empty.

The clock above her office said she was ten minutes early.

And Mandy decided there was time to relieve herself of some of the tension she had been carrying before the humdrum routine of the working week had to begin. She settled herself into her cubicle and switched on the desktop machine that dominated her workspace. After a cursory glance around the mostly empty office, Mandy pressed both hands between her thighs.

It was nearly impossible to contain the sigh of contentment.

The pressure was so needed that the slightest touch of her hand almost brought her to a rush of satisfaction. The first two fingers of her left hand teased her lips apart. The first two fingers of her right chased languid circles against her clitoris. And as she listened to the faraway sounds of her workmates entering the room and taking their places inside the surrounding cubicles, Mandy casually stroked herself to climax.

It was not an earth-shattering orgasm. A puddle of moisture stained her seat. A scent of ripe musk perfumed the immediate air of her cubicle. Mandy sighed with satisfaction.

"Are you okay, Mandy?"

She glanced up and saw Becky's concerned face peering into her cubicle. The edge of the desk covered her bare sex and stained seat. A glance at the mirror she kept by her monitor told Mandy that her features looked flushed but otherwise unremarkable. Nodding quickly, trying to conceal the naughty grin that wanted to split her lips, Mandy said, "I'm okay. The morning commute was just more demanding than I'd anticipated."

Becky rolled her eyes. In a sympathetic voice she said: "I've just spent an hour's journey getting ogled and touched up. There were two suits on the tube who couldn't keep their hands to themselves. There was one student on the bus who kept staring at my tits. And, in the lift up to this floor, I got my arse touched by that domineering bull dyke from accounts."

"Really?" Mandy gasped. "Which route do you take?"

As Becky explained the minutiae of her travel itinerary, Mandy memorized the details in readiness for her next Monday morning commute to the office. Privately, she thought it was the only thing that would make the start of the week bearable.

THIS CALL MAY BE MONITORED FOR QUALITY ASSURANCE

Xavier Acton

Rick's headset clicked, and his computer monitor flashed.

"Hello?" came the voice on the other end of the line. It was a deep, cool female voice. "Hello? Hello?"

"Hello, may I speak to...Ms. Ashley Domin...Doman..."

"Dominica," the woman said coldly. "This is she."

"Ms. Dominica, my name is Rick and I'm calling from the Term Life Insurance Company to tell you about some of the excellent products we have for you. Have you ever considered what will happen to your loved ones if you were to pass on prematurely?"

"How did you get this number?"

"Um...I'm sorry, Ms. Dominica, I don't know that."

"I prefer 'Mistress Dominica.' This number is unlisted."

"Well, Ms. Dominica, if you'll give me a moment, I can tell you about some of our excellent term life insurance products—"

"Telemarketing is very naughty."

Rick paused. "Um...well, Ms. Dominica, I would be happy

to tell you about some of our excellent term life insurance products—"

"Telemarketing is very, very, very naughty, Rick. And I told you to call me Mistress."

Rick went to say something but his throat closed up. He finally managed to squeak, "Mistress."

"Very, very naughty. Do you *like* being naughty, Rick?"

Ms. Dominica's voice was thick, rich, powerful. When she chuckled, it sounded menacing.

"Ms. Dominca, if you'd allow me to take just a moment of your time, I could tell you about some of our excellent term life insurance products—"

"Do you know what I do to little boys who are naughty, Rick? Little boys who telemarket?"

"Ummmmm…"

"Let me tell you what I use this line for, Rick. This is an unlisted number because I advertise it only in certain publications for naughty men. Those men call me and beg me to punish them. And none of them has done anything nearly as naughty as telemarketing."

Rick cleared his throat. "Ms. Dominica—"

"*Mistress* Dominica!" she snapped.

"M—M—Mistress Dominica, we've got some excellent term life insurance products—"

"I have all the insurance I need, Rick," she said. "What I *do* need, however, what I can never get enough of, is naughty little boys to spank."

"You…you really, Ms. Dominica, these really are excellent term life insurance products—"

"You're probably wearing a pair of polyester pants, aren't you? $21.99 at Sears?"

Actually, they were $24.99 at JCPenney. Rick didn't say that, though; instead, he just choked a little and gasped out, "Excellent term life insurance products."

"A thin little belt? Tighty-whities or boxers?"

"Ummmmm..."

"Boxers, I'm betting. You think they're sexier than tighty-whities, Rick, don't you?"

In fact, Rick was wearing a pair of cotton boxers with little hundred-dollar bills on them. They were a gift from his last girlfriend, who wanted to encourage him to pursue a more lucrative line of work than telemarketing.

"Boxers *are* kind of sexy, Rick. I find boxers *very* sexy."

Rick's finger hung over the Disconnect button. He could feel his cock stirring in his polyester pants, the head nudging the cotton Franklins.

"Really?" he asked weakly.

"Do you know why I like boxers on my men, Rick?"

"Ummmm..."

"Because they're easier to pull down. Do you know what I'd do to a naughty telemarketer if I had him here in my dungeon?"

"Ummmmmm..."

"I'd put you over my knee, Rick. I'd make you take your pants down and I'd put you over my knee. I'd pull down those boxers of yours and I'd run my hands all over your ass. I'd be wearing lingerie, Rick, do you like girls in lingerie? A tight little corset and a garter belt and panties?"

Rick's cock was hard all the way, sticking right through the fly of his boxers and abrading against the polyester. He tried to shift it back in, without much luck.

"I—um—term life insurance—um—products," Rick stammered.

"You know what I'd feel if you were in my lap, Rick?"

"Term, um, life insurance products..."

"No," said Ms. Dominica. "I wouldn't feel life insurance at all. I'd feel your cock. Getting hard against my thigh. As I ran my hand over your ass. And I'd know you want this, Rick. Because you know telemarketing is very naughty. Is your cock hard now?"

"Ummm…"

"That's a yes, isn't it? You know what I'd do when I felt your cock hard, Rick? I'd spank you, Rick. I'd spank your butt. I'd make you squirm in my lap. I'd spank you so hard you'd cry. But your cock would keep on getting harder and harder. Is your cock in your hand, Rick?"

Rick's hand had crept unnoticed down his belly, nearing his cock. He put it back over the Disconnect button.

"Of course not," he said.

"Put it there," she said. "Rub your cock through your pants. Because if you were here, I'd make you jerk off. Right in my lap, Rick. You'd like that, wouldn't you?"

Rick glanced around to make sure no one could see into his cubicle. He wrapped his fingers around his cock through the polyester pants and started stroking it.

"Is your cock in your hand, Rick?"

"Yes," he said.

"Yes, Mistress," she told him.

"Y—yes, Mistress."

"Then stroke it. Stroke it while I spank your ass. I want you to stroke it until you come. If you were right here with me, Rick, I'd make you stroke it until you came on my pussy. Do you know what I'd do then, Rick?"

Rick was obeying the Mistress, his hand working up and down on his cock. He was close.

"I'd make you lick it off. I'd make you lick up your own come."

"Oh, Jesus," he whispered.

"Oh, Jesus, Mistress," she growled.

"Oh, Jesus, Mistress," Rick echoed, and his cock exploded. A little grunt escaped his lips and he started to pant as his orgasm tore through him. He felt a wet stain against his fingers, soaking through his polyester pants.

"Did you come good, Rick, you naughty telemarketer?"

"Y—yes, Mistress," he rasped.

"Excellent. You'd be licking your own come off my pussy if you were here right now, wouldn't you, Rick?"

He cleared his throat. "Yes, Mistress."

"I'm going to hang up now, Rick. I want you to think about me every time you jerk off from now on. You will, won't you?"

"Yes, Mistress," Rick choked. "W...would you like me to block you from our directory, Mistress?" He was just trying to be helpful.

"I wouldn't dream of it," she said.

"Thank you for your time," he said. Then, automatically, "I forgot to notify you that this call may be monitored—"

"For your sake," said Mistress Dominica, "I hope not."

Rick glanced behind him and saw his supervisor, Ms. Carron, standing in the entrance to his cubicle, a sour look on her face. She still wore her wireless headset, and Rick noticed that she was a little flushed.

"Rick," she said. "Can I see you in my office?"

"Yes, Ms. Carron," Rick said miserably and went to get up, wondering how he could hide the wet stain in his pants.

"Not now!" Ms. Carron hissed. She leaned close to Rick and he could smell her perfume. "After work," she whispered. "Wait until everyone else has gone home."

Ms. Carron turned and left. Rick shook his head, squinting.

He took a deep breath and put his finger on the Connect button.

SEX, LIES, AND LIBRARY BOOKS

Donna George Storey

Liam had no right to be mad at me. True, I didn't let him finger my pussy in the library, but that's not a crime. It's simply being smart and keeping out of trouble. But Liam didn't see it that way. He accused me of having the imagination of a rutabaga, then jumped up from the sofa—his boner still bulging in his jeans—and left me alone to exalt in my virtue.

And contemplate the hell of a long, hot summer without sex. Or at least the kind of sex I'd been having with Liam for the past few weeks. Which was something I'd miss very much, indeed.

Liam didn't like to follow the rules. I figured that out when I practically knocked him over with the reshelving cart down in the stacks at the beginning of the summer. I'm usually more careful, but I'd just gotten chewed out by the head librarian, Mr. Petersen, and I was still reeling from the humiliation.

Liam dodged my cart with impressive grace. I wasn't quite as graceful. I opened my mouth to apologize and immediately burst into tears.

He asked me, very sweetly, what the matter was.

I was so upset, I actually told him, although at that point we only knew each other from a few shifts together at the circulation desk. Of course, he already knew about the tedious summer project for us work-study grunts: a treasure hunt for missing books that had been misshelved throughout the school year. I'd diligently worked my way through all of "anthropology" that morning, but when I reported my accomplishment to Mr. Petersen, he wasn't impressed. In fact, he told me it was supposed to take an entire week and I had to do it all over from the beginning properly.

"Petersen's an asshole," Liam replied, slipping a reassuring arm around me. "What you really need to do is learn the proper way to deal with him and his stupid project."

It might be stretching the truth to say I knew right then that I'd submit my willing body to Liam's every depraved desire, but his touch did bring a nice glow to my secret places.

His warm hand still resting on my shoulder, Liam told me his plan for the special project. He'd search his assigned section until he found three lost books—Petersen's official estimate for a shift. Then he'd go off to a corner of the library and read a novel. "Petersen told me I'm doing a fine job, by the way," he said with a grin.

It took me a moment to understand. Then I remembered seeing a dark-haired guy who looked like Liam, lounging in an armchair with *War and Peace* earlier that morning.

"Weren't you afraid you'd get caught?" I whispered, instinctively looking around for any lurking library ladies who might have overheard his mutinous scheme.

"Fuck, no. Who even comes down here in July? A couple of grad students who look more like mushrooms than humans. You should catch up on your reading, too." He picked up a

battered volume of *Lady Chatterley's Lover* from the nearest
shelf and handed it to me.

I laughed nervously. "I'm on probation with the boss
already."

"Aren't you a little old to be worried about getting a big
black mark on your permanent record?"

Liam leveled his gaze at me, and the glow between my legs
ignited into a red-hot flame of lust. I knew a dare when I heard
one. My body, at least, was itching to rise to his challenge.

This Liam guy, charming and sympathetic as he might be,
was turning out to be a bad influence.

Little did I know that that was only the beginning.

At first, our transgressions were innocent enough. We'd read
novels together in a quiet corner of C floor, then head off for
lunch at the student center. Soon we were meeting after work at
his place, too. Liam was one of those guys who could lick pussy
for hours. He said it gave him great pleasure to make me all wet
and squirmy. To be honest, I rather enjoyed it myself.

Which is why I found myself knocking on his door after
dinner that night, hoping he'd forgive me for turning him down
earlier that afternoon.

Fortunately, Liam greeted me with a big smile. When I started
to apologize, he put a finger to my lips and pulled me inside. In
an instant, he had me pressed against the wall with his body, his
fingers groping for the top button of my blouse.

It was the welcome I'd been hoping for, but for one small
detail. I pulled away. "What if your roommate comes in?"

Liam rolled his eyes. "I hate to tell you this, Melanie, but
Jack already has a pretty good idea you're not a spotless virgin.
But don't worry. He's over at his girlfriend's. They're probably
fucking in her living room as we speak."

"You act like I'm a prude or something," I protested.

Liam gave me a dubious smile. "You're not? Then let's do something wild tonight. Let's fuck right here against the wall."

"What if Jack changes his plans?" The words came out before I could stop myself.

"What are you afraid of? That you might actually have fun?"

He looked straight into my eyes. I swallowed and looked away. Maybe he was right. His crazy suggestions did scare me, but they made me hot, too.

"Hey, I know something that might help you deal with your inhibitions," he said, his voice softer. "Wait here."

He returned with a bandanna, the kind cowboy bandits wear around their mouths for a bank heist.

"What's that for?" I squeaked.

"I'm going to blindfold you. It's easier to let go in the dark."

My belly tightened, a prickle of lust mixed with fear. For all that Liam teased me about having no imagination, a crazy image suddenly flashed into my head: my own body, totally naked but for that bandanna around my eyes, facing a line of men, firing-squad style. Except instead of rifles, they were aiming their cocks at me, all purple and swollen and ready to discharge volleys of glistening...

"Well, what do you say?" he urged, interrupting my fantasy.

"Sure, I guess I could try it." I meant to sound bold and adventurous, but my voice quivered slightly.

Liam's eyes flickered with amusement. "Nah, I think you're too scared."

"Oh, yeah?" If he'd meant to make me angry, it was working. Before he could say another word, I quickly unbuttoned my blouse and unhooked my bra, shrugging them both off in a heap on the floor. Then I yanked my shorts and panties down to my ankles and kicked them across the room.

For once, I'd taken him by surprise. Liam's mouth hung open, his eyes gliding over my naked body with obvious relish.

"Put that blindfold on me," I said, pleased with my newfound tone of command.

Smiling impishly, Liam quickly tied the cloth around my eyes. To my surprise, everything suddenly was different. He hadn't even touched me yet, but my skin tingled and my pussy throbbed like a second heartbeat.

Liam grazed my ear with his lips. "Imagine we're down in the stacks. I'm going to fuck you right here, with all these books watching." He took my nipple between his fingers and twisted it gently.

Against the darkness of the blindfold, I really could see it, the two of us locked in an embrace, with books lined up on either side like rows of attentive spectators in a stadium.

"You've been waiting all day for this, haven't you?" Liam whispered.

His finger found my clit. I gasped. I *had* been waiting all day for this.

"Do it to me now. Right here in the library," I begged.

"I knew you had it in you," he said. I heard the sound of his zipper, smelled the rubbery scent of condom. Then I felt something—*down there*—Liam probing me with the head of his cock. I rose up on my tiptoes and tilted my hips forward to meet him.

He pushed into me with a soft suck of flesh.

I let out a soft moan. I'd never done it this way before. The base of his cock pressed up against my clit, each thrust rubbing me just right. I felt like a witch straddling a broomstick, ready to fly into the night. But Liam wasn't ready for takeoff yet. He slid into me with deliberate strokes, knocking my ass into the wall with a steady slap like a slow, lazy spanking.

"Do you like this? Do you like fucking naked in the stacks where someone might see you?"

"Yes," I gulped. In fact, I liked it more than I'd ever admit to him. Because the scene in my head was getting really wild. The books on the shelves swelled and shimmered, and I saw they had eyes, men's eyes, glowing with lust. And now Petersen was there, too, his bald head shiny with perspiration, his pants pooled at his ankles. As he watched us, he rubbed his cock, a huge appendage as long as a rifle.

I began to jerk my ass faster. I was close. Very close. The books leaned toward us, whispering: *Come for us, you slut. We want to see you come.*

Petersen, too, joined in the chorus. *Do the job properly this time, Melanie. Come for us. Now.*

And suddenly, as if at his command, I was, lifting up and away on my broomstick, hurtling through the sky as my orgasm blasted through me. Liam followed, grunting as he emptied himself into me.

We collapsed against each other, panting.

"That was fun," I admitted when I'd finally caught my breath.

Liam pulled off the blindfold. "It was," he agreed, "but not nearly as fun as when we really do it in the library tomorrow."

At the time, I just laughed. I knew where to draw the line.

The problem was, Liam knew just how to nudge me over.

It took him three days to convince me to fuck him in the library, actually, but in the end I couldn't say no. First of all, Liam's plan was practically foolproof. It was safest to meet in the physics annex, he said, because the serious geeks studied in the science library, and I had to admit I'd never seen another soul on C floor all summer. He also suggested I wear a skirt and no underwear to make a cover-up easier if we heard someone approaching. Finally, if any stray physicist *did* wander through, Liam swore he'd have a good story cooked up to explain what we were doing.

But there was another reason I agreed to Liam's scheme—the real reason. Ever since the night we had stand-up sex in his hallway, I couldn't stop thinking about doing it in the stacks. Even in bed with Liam, I imagined books watching us and whispering filthy words to me as I came. The only way to banish those thoughts, I figured, was to do it for real.

When the day came, everything went just as planned. Except for one glitch. As I left the circulation desk to meet Liam on C floor, Mr. Petersen came up behind me and glanced at the printout of lost books I had in my hand.

"Ah, so you'll be on the science floor today, Melanie?" he said, one eyebrow cocked as he took in my short skirt and bare legs.

"Yes, sir," I said, shivering inwardly. In spite of my fantasy, the thought of the old guy really lusting after me was less than appealing.

I mentioned Petersen's comment to Liam, but he just laughed. "He's too lazy to move his fat ass all the way down here. Come on, we've got work to do."

Eyes twinkling, he backed me up against the wall and gave me a slow, melting kiss.

"Lift your skirt," he whispered. "I know you want to show these physics nerds your naked pussy."

Heart pounding, I gathered the hem in my hands and pulled it up to my waist.

Liam stepped back to appreciate the view, as if I were some work of art he'd created. In a way, I was.

"Hurry up," I breathed. "Stick it in."

"We're demanding today, aren't we?" In spite of his bad-boy tone, he obediently pulled his hard cock out of his jeans and rolled on the rubber. In one quick thrust, he pushed himself all the way inside. I clenched my teeth, swallowing down a moan.

He began to move with aching slowness. It felt nice, almost as nice as the night in his hallway. The problem was, when I looked around the real library, there wasn't much to turn me on. The books were blank, aloof, disapproving. Petersen and his weird, oversized weapon were nowhere to be found.

Perverse as it was, I closed my eyes and pretended I was back in Liam's room. In an instant, the books leered down at me again, and Petersen was back at his post, pumping his giant tool, his eyes glued to my exposed thighs.

We're watching you, Melanie. We're watching you get fucked up against the wall.

The trick was working. I thrust my hips faster, adding a little jerk to the right to get more pressure on my swollen clit. Another minute and I was going to come in this temple of scholarly learning, skewered on Liam's cock, the baddest bad girl there ever was.

Suddenly, Liam stopped, midstroke.

"What is it?" I panted.

"I think I hear the elevator."

It took all my effort not to groan out loud. "I'm just about to come, you fuck-head. Keep going."

"We should stop, just in case." He started to pull away, but I grabbed his ass with one hand and held tight.

"Coward," I hissed.

His jaw dropped open, but I stared him down with all the fierceness of a woman on the brink of a great, big roller-coaster drop of an orgasm. Fortunately, this was a challenge he couldn't resist. He rammed into me so hard my ass knocked into the wall with a slap.

The spanking sent a fiery wave of pleasure shooting up my spine. I closed my eyes again. The books still murmured their obscenities and Petersen joined in, too, his voice almost lifelike as it echoed in my head.

Melanie?

That word was all I needed. I clutched Liam's asscheeks and pressed my face in his shoulder as I came, my body swaying with each clutching spasm.

"Melanie? Are you down here?"

I froze. Liam pulled out with a jerk, stuffing his wilting cock into his jeans.

It actually *was* Mr. Petersen calling my name.

Without thinking, I grabbed Liam's shoulders and pushed him to the floor, then curled up in a ball beside him, yanking my skirt over my bare buttocks.

"Melanie?"

Petersen's dumpy body appeared at the end of the stacks. I cringed.

"What's going on here, you two?"

I held my breath. It was Liam's cue to come to the rescue. After all, he was the master at handling the boss. Unfortunately, this time his silver tongue seemed to be tied up in a knot.

It could have been a disaster, but in a way, I have Liam to thank for helping me expose my hidden talents.

"I'm sorry, Mr. Petersen," I said in a faint, breathless voice. "It's my fault. See, I'm...I'm diabetic and I didn't eat much breakfast. We don't get paid until tomorrow and I...I had a dizzy spell. Liam was helping...."

Petersen's grim expression changed to concern. He stepped closer.

"Are you all right? Are you sure you don't need a doctor."

"Oh, no, I...I'll be okay if I just get some lunch." I smiled weakly.

The head librarian reached into his pocket and pulled out his wallet. "Here, Liam, take this girl to the student center for some food, then make sure she gets back to her room to rest. But come right back when you're finished. We need someone to cover at the circulation desk." Shaking his head, he walked back toward the elevator. "Crazy girls and their diets."

Liam's mouth hung open. I could tell he was impressed. "Hey, you're pretty good at this."

I sat up and smoothed my skirt. There were many things I could have said to him then. So who doesn't know how to handle the boss properly? Who doesn't have an imagination? Aren't you glad I took drama classes in high school and my uncle's a diabetic?

But I figured I'd be gracious with his failings, like Liam was that first day we met. So I just smiled and pulled Petersen's twenty from his hand.

"Come on, bad boy," I said. "Lunch is on me."

TAKING CARE OF BUSINESS

Sommer Marsden

S mall-minded people really piss me off. You know the ones. They've done everything. They know everything. Above all, they feel they have the right to judge everything.

That's Tricia in a nutshell. My own personal small-minded person. A chirpety little bitch who is always yammering on about something. Usually, something she knows nothing about. I could tell Tricia that I collect fossilized Egyptian cat fur balls and she would know an expert. She would own a rare fossilized cat fur ball. She would know someone with the largest collection of hardened cat hair on the planet. So, yeah, I did it on purpose. I wore the tee just to get her going. I had put up with quite enough of Tricia's shit. So I did it to be spiteful.

Sue me.

The employee appreciation dinner was for all of our hard work through the past quarter. We had done a spectacular job, according to management. Our reward? A catered cookout complete with free-flowing booze and the right to wear comfortable clothes. I wasn't too excited about spending even more time at the office, but I figured, what the hell, and went in my short denim skirt, and yes, yes, just to provoke, I wore my favorite tee. The one that says in big red letters: WHAT ARE YOU GONNA DO, SPANK ME? And on the back: OH, GOODIE!

I will cop to a zing of pleasure when Tricia read it, and I got to see her mouth pucker up into a tight little disapproving seam.

"Why would you wear that?" she hissed, and I let my eyes grow wide as if I were shocked at her reaction.

"What?"

Leo was close by. Leo leaned in and shook his coffee-colored hair out of his blue eyes and tried not to grin. He was definitely interested in this particular exchange. I shot him a quick smile and shrugged.

"That is terrible. A grown woman wearing a spanking shirt. Who would be even minutely interested in...violence in the bedroom?" She spat out the word *violence,* and I watched her fat little hands curl into even fatter little fists.

"Violence?" I echoed and felt a warm blaze of anger warm my insides. Maybe this was backfiring. Maybe I should not have provoked her. It seemed what I was really doing was provoking myself, because now I wanted to choke her until her big green eyes rolled back in her head.

"Yes. Violence!"

"Now, Tricia," Leo said, eyeing us both carefully. "I don't think spanking, especially when consensual, is the same as violence. I mean, if you want a nice hard smack on the ass, what's wrong with that?" He eyed my tee and then met my gaze and winked.

I took a deep gulp of air and realized I had been holding my breath. But Tricia shook her head vehemently and her little Shirley Temple curls swayed. I watched her down half her white zinfandel and then she eyed me up.

"You are nothing more than a tart," she said.

"Thank you," I said and accepted the beer Leo was holding out to me. "I'll see if I can find a shirt that says Tart."

Tricia sputtered and choked. I don't know what she had been expecting. Tears? For me to strip off my shirt and drop it in the nearest trash can. Be reformed. *No more spanking for me! Tricia has shown me the light.* I played with my ring and waited. I would let her hang herself if that was what she wanted. I couldn't help but wonder, though, if I would have been so calm if Leo weren't backing me up. Seeing things my way and giving me strength.

"If anyone ever tried to hit me..." she trailed off, her mouth working like a fish out of water.

"Yes?" I let the word drag out and stared her down.

"I would...I would..."

"Cry? Scream? Hit back? Come?" I dragged that word out, too, and I heard Leo suck in a breath and then chuckle lowly. At least I was entertaining him.

"That is disgusting," she growled and took a step back from me as if I were contagious. The carrier of some dreaded disease.

"To each her own," I said and took another pull on my beer. I would not let this get the better of me. There was no way.

"You are—"

"That's enough, Tricia," Leo piped in. He stood, and I realized how tall he was. How broad his shoulders were. How big his hands were and how long his fingers were. A pulse started between my legs, and I tightened my thighs to try and calm down. "You are way out of your territory here. Everyone is different. Why don't you go say hi to our boss? Mr. Jones is over there looking lost and alone. Maybe you could go kiss his ass."

Tricia opened her mouth. Closed it. Opened it again and stalked off with a murderous stride.

Leo took me by the arm and my nipples grew hard instantly. My breath froze in my throat and I felt dizzy. It was a firm and authoritative grasp. A trickle of moisture seeped from me and my panties grew damp. Damn. Why had I never really paid attention to him before?

"You did that on purpose," he said and hustled me toward the door. His voice was low and his breath was hot in my ear. He opened the door and lightly propelled me into the lobby. "You did that to get her going, but then you got yourself going, didn't you?"

He didn't necessarily sound mad—just...intense.

I started to shake my head no and realized I didn't want to lie. "Okay, I wore it because I am so sick of listening to her go on and on, day in and day out, about everything. I can't stand it when people act like all the knowledge of the universe is contained in their tiny pea brain."

I stumbled on the blue carpet as he unlocked the office door and shoved me inside. Our office was dark and silent. I could hear my breathing, harsh and raspy. I could barely make out the party chatter outside. I stood by the deserted receptionist's desk and waited.

"You should know better, Gabrielle. You are smarter than that."

I nodded. I don't know why. I just did. I agreed with everything that came out of his mouth as his blue eyes seemed to glow with muted light.

"And now, you're in trouble."

Just the words alone made my cunt flicker and constrict. My heartbeat seemed to triple in speed as a sizzle of fear shot up my spine. I swallowed and my throat clicked.

"I'm sorry," I whispered. It was so ingrained in me I didn't give it a second thought.

"Let's go."

He marched me to the copy room and flicked the lights on. The fluorescents sprang to life with an annoyed buzz. Then he hustled me forward as I tried to keep steady on my wedge sandals. The moisture between my thighs was so much worse. My heartbeat was so much faster. My body seemed to hum with electricity for what I both feared and prayed would come next.

"Lean over that copier, Gabrielle," he barked and I did.

I folded my body over the copier top, my head on the unyielding plastic. I could hear my heart beat echoing through the cover. My nipples tingled and I focused everything on not squirming like a whore. On not letting him see how very much I wanted this. Needed it.

His big hands plunged under my skirt and his callused palms cradled my ass. I bit back a moan, closed my eyes, focused on staying still. For just an instant, my body disobeyed me, and I arched back into his warm skin. Prayed for a stray finger to slide into my warm pussy. For another to play my clit like a well-loved instrument.

"Stay still," he ordered. I froze in place, held my breath. "Judging by your outfit, I'd say you're well seasoned. Any other time, I would start with ten. But for you, my little troublemaker, I say we start with twenty."

My cunt clutched around nothing. Greedy and ready. All the man said was "twenty" and my body went soft and molten right there.

My white lace thong was discarded with no fanfare, and again I fought the urge to wiggle my ass at him. To blatantly ask for my punishment. It took everything I had not to move.

The first blow fell without warning. There was no shift in

the air, no electrical charge. It simply landed with a sharp sound like a twig breaking, and a flower of fire bloomed on my skin. The next was just as unexpected. I bucked against the copier as my body responded to the pain with a flood of pleasure. I would have given anything for the permission to touch myself. To ram a few fingers inside my body, to stroke my clit. But I would never ask and he would never let me.

By ten, my body was vibrating. I could feel the welts rising. There was no light touch, no playful swats. This was truly a punishment. I was being taken to task for provoking a coworker.

"Twelve," Leo growled and I felt his big fingers slide into me. I let out a groan as he fucked me with his fingers. I stayed as still as humanly possible because if I didn't, I knew damn well he would stop. He curled his fingers deep inside of me. Stroked over the most sensitive spots until my knees felt weak and my head felt like it would float away. But he never missed a blow.

"Sixteen!" he grunted. His voice was harsh with the effort of his hands. Each blow sent me closer, and then I heard his zipper and I nearly came from the sound. He nudged me with the head of his cock, opened me wide with his fingers, and drove into me. My breasts slammed the copier lid as he started hard, fast strokes. I lost count.

I clutched at the hinged plastic, pushing back against him as he fucked me harder. I distantly heard the electronic doorbell sound of the suite being entered. The final blow landed and he sighed in my ear: "Good girl. Good girl. It is good to take your punishment."

His fingers bit into my hips and his cock banged into me. I wanted to tell him of the sound I had heard but I was lost to that. I didn't care. All I cared about was the feel of him in me and the sweet, unfolding pleasure that was turning my body to fire. He stroked my clit with one big finger, applying just the right amount of pressure until I sang out loudly. I came, letting my head hit the copier and my body go limp as he followed close behind. One final thrust and a noise that wasn't even human.

Then the sounds of our breathing. That and soft footfalls just outside the door.

"Up with you," he whispered in my ear and pulled me back against him. He kissed the back of my neck and it felt like he had branded me with his hot lips. I looked around for my panties but they were nowhere to be found. Someone would have a surprise come Monday morning.

I straightened my skirt, letting my palms run briefly over the swollen, blazing skin of my cheeks. I was water, fire, wind, and air. I felt formless.

Leo whipped open the door. Tricia's pale, startled face greeted us.

"She was rude, Tricia," he said. "Don't worry. I've taken care of business." Then he winked and walked past her.

Tricia's mouth popped open as she looked to me. No doubt my face was flushed a charming pink, my hair disheveled, and my eyes glassy. The look a woman gets when she has been good and thoroughly fucked.

"Sorry, Tricia," I mumbled and bit back a laugh.

Leo took my arm and, making sure he could be heard, said, "We're not done. I'll be taking you home."

It wasn't a question.

I nodded, then turned back and smiled for Tricia. Thank God for small-minded people.

HOW TO FUCK YOUR BOSS

Elizabeth Young

After bending him over the desk, I peer into the asshole of my boss, wondering, and not for the first time, whether my obvious predilection for self-destruction is more a fetish than a character flaw. There is a trace of the ridiculous in all of this, and by the time I am moistening the tip of my finger, I am not at all surprised that our working relationship has crossed the line. After all, what's the use of screwing your boss up the ass if not for the chance to ruin your career? So here I am, aimed for insertion, staring at his business-casual khakis puddling around his ankles and wondering if I could still show some grace and walk out the office door, when he pushes himself back toward me.

Well, here we go.

His ass is as I expected—shiny and buffed, clean with not a trace of hair left in the crack—and I run my finger up and down it, feeling the silky smoothness. My tongue darts out of my mouth on instinct. As I press a finger against his opening, he puckers up and I slide into him, the tip of my finger entering him slowly, getting him used to me and the rhythm of being fucked.

He takes to it the way all thirty-something middle managers do. Easy. Somewhere wired in the back of their brains is a spot that says: *Yes. Anal finger fucking is just fine by me. But only if it's done by an underling who is smarter and not well paid.*

His breath quickens as I slide in and out, his cock, rock hard, bounces over the lip of the desk, oozing honey from the slit and soaking the tail ends of his dress shirt. I slip in another finger, stretching him open, and feel the muscles tighten around me as I break him in.

"Harder," he grunts pushing himself down my fingers until he settles onto my knuckles, his ass hungrily sucking on me, pulling at me to go deeper, fuck him harder. And just as he gets going, I pull out of him.

"Good boy, now get on your knees," I say, as he lowers himself in front of me. There is nothing in the world more beautiful than a man on his knees. "Now, love, go to work," I tell him, raising my skirt high enough to give him an idea.

He slides his hands beneath my skirt, pushing it up over my hips. I feel him brush against my skin as he tucks the fabric into my waistband. Leaning forward, he is poised to go in, and I slap him hard across his face. "I didn't tell you to touch me yet."

Perhaps we should take a moment and reflect that I just bitch-slapped my boss for no apparent reason other than I've decided to go ahead and lose my mind.

I pause, expecting the firing that is bound to come next. Instead, he simply sits back and smiles.

Perhaps I was wrong about him after all.

I let him wait until I can't stand it, and I push his face into me, rubbing myself around his mouth and nose. Imagining that tongue of his inside me, licking me from clit to ass, is enough to soak my panties and his face. I can feel his chin opening up my cunt from the pressure I am putting on him. It feels so good and I ache to feel a little pain.

"Rip my panties off."

Always go with the classics.

He grabs hold of my knickers, trying to tear the fabric away from me, but instead of ripping, the fabric stretches and screams against my skin, biting into me, rubbing the flesh away from my belly.

"Use your teeth—eat them off me."

He pushes his face back into me, his teeth grabbing hold of the fabric near my thigh. He pulls back, fabric in teeth, sawing through my panties until they rip away from the elastic near the leg hole. He lets go, my panties snap back against me, and his tongue snakes through the hole in the fabric, running up and down my skin. He draws the fabric away from me, his nails dragging through my pubic hair, until the whole front of my panties is ripped away, exposing my wet cunt.

He waits, hovering near the heat growing from between my legs, his tongue darting between his lips, wanting to dive in, and still I don't say a word. It's punishing to have him so close, feeling his breath on me. I want him to do it, forgetting to wait for me to say it's okay. I can feel him going forward into me before he even moves, and then he does. His tongue parts my lips and slips inside the fold, the tip exploring me, pushing into me, tentatively at first, then suddenly sliding in, making my knees give, and he has to hold me up, balanced by his tongue.

And we're off.

Thoughts go through my head at lightning speed: *What am I doing here? A little to the right. Did I feed the cat this morning? Did I back up the file? Oh. My. God. That's right, harder. Don't forget to get milk...*

He pushes me against the same desk that I had him on, and

I lean back, my ass on the lip of it pushing his face into me. His fingers slide up to my clit and push away the hood of skin that hides it. He draws his tongue out of my pussy and up to my clit, circling, sucking, until I feel like I am about to die. I am so close to coming that my cunt feels like a freight train.

He pulls away from me and stands up. I try to hit him for leaving me on the edge. He catches my hand and bends my arm behind me, his body pressing up against mine.

"Turn around," he says and I do. The roles reverse effortlessly. He lets go of my arm, and I face the desk, my hands on the top of it to steady myself. Bending me over, he kicks my legs wide apart, then runs his hand over my ass and down to my clit. He slides two fingers inside me, drawing out my own honey and coating my thighs with it until I am dripping. He rubs his cock against me, oiling the head and quickly replaces his fingers with himself, slamming into me. I raise up on my toes and he starts to fuck me slowly, slipping all the way out and ramming back in. I bite my lip hard and feel the moans bubble up from the back of my throat.

He pulls out of me and reaches into the desk drawer to pull out a condom. He rolls it over his prick and spreads open my cheeks. I am so wet that he slides into me easily. He pumps, his balls smashing up against the back of my thighs. He reaches around and sticks his fingers inside my cunt, the heel of his hand pressing into my clit, rocking me back and forth until I can't stop myself from screaming out loud.

"So," he says when we untangle ourselves, "do you think you can finish up the Laraby file tomorrow?"

I plan to call in sick.

HEADHUNTER

CB Potts

Y ou've been with Langston Brothers quite a while now."
Meredith eyed me speculatively over her martini. Her eyes
were deep green, with flecks as dark as the olive.

"Four years." My drink sat untouched. It would taste too
good after the day I'd had. Yet another accounting scandal had
broken, sending herds of nervous investors skittering from one
fund to another. Twelve hours with a phone in my ear, moving
hundreds of thousands of shares over a computer system determined to freeze up every twenty minutes.

At the end of the chaos, an invitation for drinks with a
midlevel exec from Sullyman. Not exactly our competition—
they were a fraction of the size of Langston—but close. Close
enough that we were meeting in a tiny club halfway across the
city, far from prying eyes.

Usually, I don't accept these kinds of invitations. Nine times
out of ten, they're from young up-and-comers who want an
inside track to working at Langston. But this was different.

Meredith hadn't sounded hungry. She was calm and confident, and although I was ashamed to admit it, her voice was sexy as hell. Hoping that her appearance matched the voice, I'd agreed.

She hadn't disappointed. Meredith was short and blond—my two favorite features in one package. Thin enough that she must visit a gym but not anorexic enough to get her mail there. She even smelled good, a subtle scent of summer citrus trailing her. Best of all, she was smart. Very smart. Three syllables out of her mouth, and I knew Meredith wasn't here for the ambiance. Something was up, and I wanted my head clear while I found out what it was.

"A long time." She signaled the waiter. Perfectly manicured nails. Short, perfectly manicured nails.

"Not that long."

"Long enough that you should be running a division now, instead of working for Ron Coleman." Blond hair tucked behind a tiny ear, revealing a decent-sized diamond stud. "How do you stand it?"

"Ron's very bright." I sipped at my drink, cool gin chasing the bitter taste in my throat. "I've learned a lot from him."

"If you haven't mastered walking on the back of your subordinates and taking credit for all their work after four years, when are you going to get it?" She finished her drink in one long swallow and signaled for another. "I figured him out in three months."

"Good for you." I smiled thinly, glancing around the room for an exit. "And yet I'm making twice as much money as you. How strange is that?"

"Half as much." Meredith smiled. "But it doesn't have to be that way."

"Excuse me?"

She leaned toward me, resting pinstriped elbows on the

tablecloth. The watch peeking from beneath the French cuffs was real. No rings on the fingers clasped under her chin.

"You're making half as much money as you could be. We're familiar with Langston, and even with a generous year-end bonus, you're not going to earn fifty percent of what we're willing to pay you."

Cradling my glass between wide-splayed fingers, I said, "You're talking about half a million dollars."

Meredith laughed. "Nice try. We're talking about three hundred thou—plus more chances for advancement than you'll ever get at Langston."

"Because I'm Chinese?" Sullyman's Pacific Rim division had been doing well lately. Very well.

"Because you're talented as hell. We watched the O'Hare purchase. It took balls to route that through Kenya. Not many traders would have sent that much money into Africa."

I smiled. "I have a soft spot for emerging market equity."

"You've got a soft spot for girls, too, I hear." Meredith leaned closer and dropped her voice to a whisper. "That's why you've had the same desk for four years."

"If you say so," I said, sipping from my drink. There was merit in what she said. Langston's conservative values were well known. "But that shouldn't be an issue."

"Shouldn't be, but it is." Her eyes locked with mine. "The fact you haven't dated anyone in two and a half years doesn't mean that they'll forget you're queer."

My relationship with Rina had hardly been public knowledge, much less its dissolution. It was my turn to lean closer. "How long have you been watching me?"

"Professionally, about four months." Meredith looked away. "Personally, ever since Rina moved in with my ex."

"I wish her luck. Rina's an expensive girl."

Meredith laughed. "There's some kind of justice in that. Carolyn could spend faster than I could earn."

"What's happening to your money now?"

Green eyes came back, locked with mine. A blond eyebrow cocked upward just a fraction.

"I keep it."

"Then you can spring for the room."

Even more discrete than the restaurant, the motel offered few amenities beyond the heavily draped windows, an industrial-size bed, and off-street parking. That was fine. We weren't there as Michelin researchers.

"Is this part of every job offer Sullyman makes?" I asked.

Meredith chuckled. "Only if we're recruiting an incredibly hot dyke...."

Conversation died as she slid the blazer from my shoulders. I reached for her, eager to see what I'd been speculating about all evening, but she stopped me.

"Let me. You're the guest."

Her fingers flew over the buttons of my blouse, easing the silk to the floor. My skirt followed, sliding down with a whispered caress. Admittedly prosaic lingerie fluttered away, soft blue butterfly scraps drifting to the carpet.

"You're even more beautiful than I'd imagined," Meredith whispered. An evil grin raced across her face. "And I can imagine quite a bit."

Only then did we kiss—me completely naked, her fully clothed. Her mouth was martinis and expensive teeth, perfectly smooth and even under my tongue. She wrapped her hands in my hair, holding my head the entire time we kissed, soft palms covering my ears.

"Lie back," she directed.

I sprawled on the bed, brown eyes wide as Meredith shed her clothes. She didn't undress, exactly. She writhed out of her garments, shimmying her hips out of well-cut slacks to reveal a lacy black thong.

I raised an eyebrow. "I see you were prepared for this encounter."

"Let's just say I had hopes," she replied. There was a matching bra, of course, cradling her small round breasts into the barest suggestion of cleavage. I wanted to free them, touch and taste them, but Meredith had other plans.

Her first kiss was a half-inch above my left ankle, on the inside of my leg. Her lips felt like fire, as caress by caress, peck by peck, she worked her way up.

I was panting by the time she reached my knee.

"Patience," she murmured. "We've got all night." One arm wrapped around my thigh, holding me in place. I could feel her tongue tracing secret messages on my skin, writing out words of anticipation and desire forestalled.

"Please," I whispered.

Every inch of my body was covered in a cold sweat, every inch that wasn't burning red hot from the touch of her hand, the soft brush of her lips. My hips were rising up off the bed of their own volition, begging for attention.

I felt her smile against the very top of my thigh. Her hair was brushing over my mound, golden strands sliding through sparse black curls.

She cupped her hands under my ass, lifting my pelvis up and staring for a split second. "Absolutely beautiful."

Then she bowed her head.

Her tongue was so hot, a perfectly focused firebrand carving through my folds. She swirled around, lapping like a starving cat. Delicious friction rasped against my clit, bearing down hard one moment, feather light the next.

My legs were shaking. She wrapped one arm around each thigh without missing a beat, keeping her face buried in the center of my universe. Noises I thought I'd forgotten were pouring out of my mouth—deep, throaty moans, pleas to a deity who seldom turned her face my way.

Yet Meredith kept on, plunging her tongue deep inside me, an extremely talented surrogate cock demanding entry. I thrust my hips up to meet every jab, daring her to give me more, grinding into her chin.

I could feel the climax building, pleasure welling deep inside. Long-neglected nerve endings rejoiced in a paroxysm of joy, sending electric shocks throughout my body. I shook like a feather in a hurricane.

And then, ever so gently, Meredith pressed her lips together over my clit, sandwiching it firmly inside her mouth.

The flood gates opened. Wave after wave of orgasm coursed through me, sending me farther over the edge than I'd ever been before. I'm surprised the cops didn't show up. My screams were so loud they must have heard me in space.

Meredith knelt on the edge of the bed. "I'm guessing that all means you had a good time."

"Come here," I said, pulling her down next to me. The thong was gone in a second, ripped away to reveal the golden fringe of her bush. She was already wet, the heady smell of her arousal mingled with the citrus overtones of her perfume.

She was liquid velvet, smooth and hot at the same time, twisting underneath me. All the while I could hear her panting, "More, more, more," and so I obliged, licking and slurping through her screams.

My fingers slid in easily, twisting in her heat as I nuzzled at her clit.

Her orgasm came quicker than mine—perhaps she was more practiced—but it was no less quiet. I was pinned between her thighs, my nose to the grindstone, as she flailed through a tremendous climax.

The glow died slowly, leaving us lying side by side in a silent room, breathing in time.

Meredith rolled up on her elbow and took one long strand of my black hair between her fingers. "Not to mix business with some rather superlative pleasure, but do I have any chance of luring you to Sullyman?"

"That depends," I said, crossing one arm behind my head. "Any chance of getting that offer up to three and a half?"

Meredith burst out laughing. "You are too much." She rolled on top of me, nudging my thighs apart with her knee. "But considering your...specialized skill set," she smiled, "I'm sure that could be arranged."

LATE FOR WORK

Shelly Jansen

I was late for work. Again. I could feel Marcus watching me, and when I looked over at him, I saw him smiling at me. "You're like a cartoon," he grinned. "Moving in fast motion." He likes to watch me get ready for my day, even when I'm not in a rush. But when he tried to corner me in the bedroom and kiss the back of my neck, I shrugged him away.

"I'm late—" I insisted, pointing to the clock on the nightstand. I was almost ready to go. I only had to finish doing my makeup.

Marcus looked longingly at me with his dark-brown eyes. "Never too late for a kiss. Right, baby?"

"Right," I agreed, setting down my lipstick. I would never trade a kiss with Marcus for anything, and I relaxed enough to let him embrace me. Marcus took full advantage of the situation. While he bit my bottom lip, he traced the mother-of-pearl buttons running down the front of my silk shirt, then gently ran his fingertips over my full breasts. My nipples grew instantly hard, and I had to force myself to stay focused on the time.

"We'll have fun tonight," I told him. "I promise. I'll be all yours then."

"Five minutes, Nicole," he begged, taking my hand and placing it on the crotch of his jeans. "Just five minutes."

"I can't," I insisted. As I spoke, the front bell rang. "That's Carla. She's picking me up today."

"I know she is," Marcus said, confusing me. I didn't remember telling him. Usually, I meet Carla at her apartment. But I couldn't think about that right then, because Marcus had his hands wrapped in my long dark hair, and he pulled me firmly to his strong chest, in a tight, bear hug. I could feel his impressive morning hard-on through his faded blue jeans, and my resolve to be a good little employee wavered dangerously until the front bell rang again. I was going to have to change my panties before heading out to work. Marcus's kiss had made me all wet.

"I *have* to go." I sprinted down the hall to the door, with Marcus trailing after me. I'd have Carla wait in the living room while I went back to the bedroom and chose a new thong. That was my plan. As I opened the front door, I heard Marcus laughing softly behind me.

"That's a fairly snazzy look, Michelle." Carla grinned at me. "Although I'm not sure it's appropriate for work. *Even* on casual Friday." She raised her mirrored shades up to anchor her streaked blond hair out of her eyes, and she kept on smiling at me in the most disconcerting fashion. I didn't know what she was talking about. But then I felt the cool morning breeze against my naked skin and looked down at myself.

"Marcus!" I shouted, blushing as I tried to cover myself up. While we'd been kissing in the bedroom, he'd unbuttoned my blouse. My shirt was open to midwaist, revealing both my lacy pink bra and my flat stomach, well toned from hours of crunches.

"Were you going to let me leave for work looking like this?"

"You look beautiful," Carla told me, taking a few steps forward and closing the door behind her. I turned to glance back at her, surprised at the husky tone of her voice. Was it my imagination, or was she dressed rather sexily herself? She had on a pastel-pink dress that hugged her curves. Her long legs were bare, and she'd chosen to complete her outfit with tie-up, rose-colored espadrilles. "Absolutely beautiful," she repeated.

"That's what I thought," Marcus agreed. Slowly, they moved around me, like animals circling for the kill, and I started to feel certain that something was going on that I didn't know about. When Marcus grabbed me from behind and Carla came forward to kiss my parted lips, I knew that I was right. That didn't stop me from pressing my lips to my pretty coworker's and giving into the desire building within me. Again, I could feel Marcus's erection, but now he was pressing his rocklike cock firmly against my ass. I was so wet that I thought I might melt right there between the two of them. When Carla started to caress my breasts as she kissed me, I sighed hard. Her fingertips were maddeningly light. I longed to have her touch me harder, to feel her hands cupping my breasts, squeezing them firmly as we made out.

"We're going to be late—" I stammered when we parted, as if that were the most important thing. *As if.* Here I was, half-naked, kissing a coworker while my boyfriend happily participated.

"We're not going to work today," Carla said matter-of-factly as she set her sunglasses down on our living room end table.

"We're not?"

"No, you're not," Marcus repeated.

I looked now to gaze at Marcus, who was regarding me with one of his trademark sexy smirks. He had his hands all over me now, carefully undoing the rest of the buttons on my blouse.

Then he undid the snap of my bra, as if for good measure.

"Exactly what's going on?" I murmured dumbly, catching my lacy bra in my hands and then cradling my arms in front of my naked breasts. I felt dizzy and exposed, as if I were in a dream. This wasn't a bad feeling at all, I realized to my surprise, and when Carla went to her knees and began unzipping the zipper at the side of my skirt, I didn't say a word. I simply watched her part the navy blue fabric and slide the expensive skirt down my long, slim thighs. Her fingers on me set my skin on fire, even through my stockings.

"You know that secret fantasy you confessed to me the other night?" Marcus asked, pulling my arms open and taking my shirt off me.

Of course, I knew, but my cheeks flamed up anyway at the memory. First, we'd shared a half-bottle of red wine and then we'd shared X-rated fantasies. Luckily, ours meshed. He wanted to experience a ménage à trois with me and another girl, and I wanted to invite my beautiful friend Carla to join us in the bedroom. Even as I whispered my desires, I knew I'd never have the nerve to bring this moment to reality. But apparently Marcus had.

"I called us in sick," Carla explained from her position at my feet. She looked up at me approvingly, stroking her finger-tips along the lacy tops of my garters. They were one of my sexiest sets, and I was secretly glad that I'd chosen to wear them today. "Said that we'd been up working on the Miller project last night and that we'd worn ourselves ragged. I promised we'd have the file in first thing Monday morning. Ms. Delacorte was very reasonable when I told her we'd be working through the weekend without overtime."

"You did all that without me knowing?" I asked, stating the obvious, but I didn't really care about her answer. She was now on her knees with her face pressed to my panty-clad pussy, and in a second, her tongue had flicked out to touch my clit. I felt suddenly off-balance, but Marcus was right behind me, supporting me as Carla licked my pussy through my pretty panties. Her warm breath and her wet tongue sent sparks through me, even through the fabric barrier, and I desperately wanted to feel her kissing my naked skin. Marcus must have sensed my unspoken desires, because he brought me over to our large red sofa and motioned for Carla to come with us. In moments, I was spread out and Carla was nestled between my thighs, pulling my knickers down. I gasped as I felt her part my nether lips with her fingers and then bring her mouth to my waiting pussy. I leaned my head back against one of our soft cushions, and I closed my eyes, but Marcus would have none of that.

"Look at me," he whispered, and I automatically obeyed his command, opening my eyes and staring up at him as Carla continued to treat me to the most delicious pussy-licking I could imagine. She parted my lips so wide that I felt an ache deep within myself, a good ache that made me crave anything she had to give. Then she brought her mouth directly to my clit, ringing it with her lips while her tongue flicked out to tap on it again and again. I squirmed and moaned, reveling in every sensation. Carla seemed to know exactly how to touch me. She teased me with her tongue around my clit, not touching it directly, and then she rapped on it firmly and I felt myself spiraling with pleasure.

God, did it feel amazing—but then suddenly I wanted more.

"I want to taste you," I said, reaching my fingers down to touch her sun-streaked curls. "Please."

Carla was quick to oblige. She stood and shed her dress in a single motion, and I sucked in my breath when I saw that she was entirely naked under that pale-pink sheath. "I came prepared," she smiled, cocking her hip in a model's pose. She was clean shaven, her pussy totally bare, and she looked as if she'd just stepped off a nude beach on some tropical fantasy island. Her skin gleamed, warm and golden in the morning sunlight. I was ravenous just looking at her, and I was thrilled when she moved back to the sofa and climbed on top of me in a sultry sixty-nine.

I had never tasted a woman's pussy before, but I didn't hesitate. I felt Marcus's eyes watching as I used my thumbs to spread her lips and then brought my tongue carefully to her clit. I worked softly at first, tentatively, I guess, until Carla said: "Harder, Nicole. Let me feel it."

That gave me the freedom to flutter my tongue firmly against her clit. Her juices spread quickly to my lips and cheeks, and I adored the glossy sensation of being drenched in her most erotic liquids. I paid attention to what she was doing between my own legs, and I worked to mirror every motion. I drank from her, then ran my tongue in random circles around her clit.

When I turned my head slightly, I saw Marcus sitting in the easy chair opposite from us, his jeans spread open, his hand on his throbbing cock. He was transfixed, and I could tell he was loving every minute. My heart beat faster at the sight of him watching us. I realized we were putting on a show for him, even as we were reveling in our own enjoyment. I couldn't decide which concept was sexier...but then I had to stop thinking and focus my attention on the prize in front of me, licking and lapping as Carla worked to bring me to orgasm.

I didn't sense it before it happened. All of a sudden, I was just coming, hard and furious, bucking against her. As I came, I continued to suck on her clit, as if it were a piece of hard candy, and my actions helped her reach her own climax, so that we were coming together, like one being, joined and connected.

Carla came quietly, which surprised me. I thought she might be a screamer, crying out at the moment of her peak. But no, she was nearly silent, her body shaking with the power of her orgasm. For some reason, the contained way that she came made me even more aroused. I had a desire to break her down, to make her scream next time. And I knew the next time would be coming soon.

We lay there shuddering on the couch for several moments, breathless and dazed, until I could finally speak again.

"Marcus," I said softly, "let's go to the bedroom. We need more space."

Our sexy trio headed quickly down the hall. I was first, naked except for my garters and stockings. I had Carla's hand in mine, and I pulled her along after me. Marcus trailed behind us, and when I looked over my shoulder, I saw he was shedding his clothes on the journey. By the time we reached our room, he was naked except for his blue-and-white-striped boxers. Carla and I didn't say a word. It was as if we had planned this ahead of time. We grabbed Marcus and pushed him back on the bed. Then she pulled his boxers off and threw them in a corner. I could tell from the expression on Marcus's face that he liked being stripped by a lady.

I climbed on one side of him, and she took the other. While I started to suck his ever-so-hard cock, she began to tickle his balls with the tip of her tongue. I imagined what her long, soft hair must feel like against his naked skin, and I thought of the two of us girls pressing our breasts against him, touching him in similar ways, echoing each other.

Marcus moaned and arched his back, and I took that as a sign to change positions with my friend. Then, she started to bob up and down on his cock while I bathed his balls in the warm, wet heat of my mouth.

"Oh, girls," he sighed, his whole body trembling. "Oh, my girls—"

"He's ready," Carla murmured to me, and then she raised her blond eyebrows, asking a silent question. I nodded and immediately she climbed astride his straining hard-on. Marcus's eyes held mine as Carla started to ride him. I gazed at my man as long as I could, but then I found myself too captivated by Carla's body. I knelt at her side and started to lick her nipples, first one, then the other. Then I pinched them both between my fingers and thumbs, and she groaned and pumped harder up and down on Marcus's cock.

"You come here," he said, grabbing for me. Soon I was straddling his mouth while facing Carla. We were both astride him, both taking our pleasure from his body. Marcus teased my ripe clit with his tongue and teeth while Carla stroked her fingers along my ribs and up to my breasts. She and I leaned forward and started to kiss each other, and I thought I might lose all control then. We made the perfect triangle, a fantasy creation, with Marcus thrusting his cock into her pussy and his tongue into mine. I was awash in erotic shivers, my whole body on fire, when Carla said, "Switch!"

Moving from my front-row seat was heartbreaking. I had to pull my pussy away from Marcus's delicious mouth and tantalizing tongue, but then I saw his glistening cock so ready for me, and I couldn't wait to impale myself on it. I had him between my thighs in seconds, while Carla took over my former position, with her pussy poised over my man's waiting mouth.

We started up again, and I felt the climax building within me, making it hard for me to breathe. I was so turned on by watching my tan and nubile friend growing more aroused by the moment, and I was filled to overflowing with Marcus's cock. I don't think he'd ever been this hard before.

"I'm going to—" I started to say.

"Don't you dare," Carla insisted. "We'll all come together. That's how it should be. You wait until Marcus is ready."

"Are you?" I hissed. "Are you, Marcus?"

His reply was muffled against Carla's cunt, but I could tell he said, "Yes."

"Now?" I asked Carla. "Are you ready?" My voice bordered on the desperate. I didn't think I could hold back much longer. What if she said no? What if she told me to wait?

To my great relief, she said: "Yes. Now, Nicole. Now, sweetheart. Now!"

I ground my hips against Marcus, and I could feel him come inside of me. Each thrust, each pump of his hips against mine brought me higher. But then I remembered how Carla had come before. So silent. Everything inward. This time, I wanted her to make noise, and I told her so.

"Come loud," I said. "For me. Let me hear it."

She locked on my eyes then, watching me so fiercely as those amazing tremors rumbled through me. As if gaining strength from me, she parted her lips and the most musical moans issued forth. "Oh, Nicole," she whispered.

"Louder!"

"Nicole!" she cried out, and the sound of her untamed voice made me come like a powerhouse. As those magical vibrations beat through me, Carla leaned forward one more time and kissed me, and, joined like that, the three of us came together.

For several moments, nobody spoke. Then Carla slid over to Marcus's side. She ran her fingertips up and down her own body as she gazed at me. I pulled off Marcus and found a place at his other side, sandwiching him between us. The three of us stayed like that, warm and satisfied in the center of the bed. Then Carla looked over at the clock on the nightstand.

"Think of all those people at their desks now," she giggled.

"Or rushing in," Marcus said, "late for work." He tickled me, and I started to laugh, remembering how out of control I'd been at the start of the morning, hurrying while he watched. That whole time, he'd known that my rush was futile and that his secret plans would kick into effect any moment.

"But we have nothing else to do all day but fuck," Carla said, leaning over Marcus to kiss me firmly on the lips.

"And remember," Marcus said from below us, "you two are supposed to put in a lot of overtime this weekend."

"Oh, yeah," Carla said, giggling again. This time I joined her, and the three of us repeated the word together: "Overtime."

IN THE EMPIRE
OF LUST

Maxim Jakubowski

I have a corner office. The view is nothing special, though. The grime of the London rooftops unfolding nearby and the gray, teeming streets of borderline Soho below are quite unremarkable. Although the company where I work occupies the third floor of the building, it also happens to be the top floor, so the panorama I'm afforded is limited and tedious. No Thames unfurling below, no romantic or historical city milestones to contemplate when my mind goes on a random walkabout away from the bulging files accumulating across my desk or the flickering screen of the see-through iMac I use.

And my mind certainly wanders a lot these days. Too much. Much too much. A good thing I'm management. Such absent-minded moods would not be cause for forgiveness if I were at a more junior level. But then I wouldn't occupy a corner office.

I usually keep my door open so staff outside have access to me. Good management, I'm told, but it's actually more due to the fact I'd just feel so damn lonely, isolated in my cocoon of an office had I no contact with the outside, the swish of skirts out there, the sweet voices of women gossiping, the other telephones ringing when mine insists on remaining silent. Thinking is a lonely affair. And thinking is what they pay me for, I suppose.

But then I cheat. For every crassly remunerated thought of advertising campaigns and slogans and clever ways of convincing the punter out there to greedily consume more orange- or chocolate- or strawberry-flavored ice cream or instant desserts with disconcerting tastes, I also indulge in private moments, secret thoughts that have little to do with my job. My world inside the world.

Veronica brings me a dossier she wishes me to check. She is pear-shaped but always has such a wonderful smile. And a great arse. A backside that inspires me mightily. Outlined against the fabric of her skirt by her highly visible panty line. Some days, I know, she wears thongs and my imagination runs riot, delineating the undoubtedly pale and hard flesh of her joyful arse and guessing what shades of pink I could impose on its regal expanse, smacking her there hard and sharp as she thrusts her backside toward me while prone in a doggie position, the puckered hole of her anus winking at me and the humid cut of her gash opening oh so slightly. Veronica's backside is such a tempting invitation to mark with the fleeting print of my hand.

Enough to make a fetish freak of me, by temperament such a vanilla sort of gentle pervert!

And then there's Suzanne, of the long, dark blond hair that unrolls all the way down to the small of her back and of the shy, tentative interventions at our weekly creative meeting. She has thick, pulpy lips that beg for a terrible object to cradle obscenely right in their geographical center. A penis, maybe? Mine? On her knees in front of me, my gaze descending on the razor-straight part that divides her silky hair. Her tongue emerging quite hesitantly from the scarlet flower of those lips before inevitably tasting the rough texture of my bulging, blood-engorged glans before she courageously ingests it all in one full, hungry movement and my cock lodges itself like an Amazon explorer down deep in her throat. Suzanne's face speaks of both innocence and knowing, but I wouldn't be surprised if her cocksucking skills were on a par with the welcome instances of lateral thinking she often displays in her job. At the meetings, I am hypnotically drawn to her lips as the digestive biscuits she feasts on invariably breach her threshold. Her desk sits just to the right of the exit to my office. The window behind her chair enjoys the same view as I do. Limited and uninspiring. Maybe in her private world of office work, Suzanne also dreams of a world of blow jobs.

Polly calls me on the phone. Her own office is only at the other end of the corridor, but she prefers to communicate this way. She is in charge of promotions. Her eyes are brown and slightly Asian. She is one-quarter Malaysian on her mother's side, I know. Polly is always on the go, a hive of activity, thin as a rake, small perky breasts with nipples ever erect and visible, shape-wise, through her T-shirts or cashmere sweaters. She is always brimming with confidence, but I sense it's only a shell, a wafer-thin display of assurance and that, deep in her heart, she is an insecure little girl who privately begs for submission in one-to-one relationships.

Wouldn't she just look perfect with a leather studded dog collar or a Vivienne Westwood choker tightened around her neck? A docile lass I would pull with a leash into the room full of people and present as my slave for all to feast upon at their leisure. "Display yourself," I would order, and she would shed her coat and reveal her total nudity beneath the protective garment. Her nipples would be delicately pierced, thin gold rings standing to attention. Her cunt would be shaved smooth, and when another party guest would summarily order her to open her legs wide (and no need for a spreader bar, she is such an obedient lass), the diamond stud fixed to her clitoral hood would miraculously emerge from the gates of her labia, already coated with her fragrant, inner juices. *So what will the slave have to perform today?* she wonders, both quite ashamed at her situation and predictably aroused and obediently submissive. All Polly wishes to know on the occasion of this phone call, however, is if I have yet agreed on the budget for the soft drinks project whose pitch our team is working on, and to which accounting code the development expenses should be allocated.

Jasmine, my deputy, walks in, her long legs sliding across the regulation carpet of the office, and perches herself shamelessly across the corner of my desk, unveiling more square inches of thigh than an older executive would tolerate, and painstakingly explains to me how the art department has once again misunderstood the specifications for a particular job and we are running late. As if didn't already know this. But she reassures me: she will stay on late today and keep an eye on Frank, our gay art director, and see that he doesn't leave until the boards are ready for the presentation. She wears old-fashioned glasses and speaks in clipped Oxbridge tones. I know she is seeing an Australian graphic designer she met in a bar some months back and that this is the first proper relationship she has had in well over a year. My eyes linger on the stockinged legs draped over my desk and, Superman-like, explore beyond. She always wears white knickers, and I've often had a flash of them. Below the cotton or the silk, I imagine her pubic hair is dark and curly and her cunt is tight and dry. But when she is fucked, she comes loud and hysterically, her whole body vibrating to the rhythm of the thrusts of the cock frantically buried inside her and tears forming in the corner of her pale green eyes. Yes, I reckon

Jasmine must be quite beautiful in the embrace of pleasure, relinquishing all her civilized and reserved façade and reverting to a blissful state of sluttishness under the mere touch of a man's hand exploring her skin and mapping its soft contours. I thank her most sincerely for her attention to detail and feel my cock growing insidiously inside my black trousers, under the shelter of the desk. Watching her lips move and catching a brief glimpse of her white brassiere, I suddenly have a revelation that deep down inside her universe of secrets Jasmine actually likes having a cock up her arse when her passion grows out of passion. However, sometimes you just know these things, intuition and all that, it also came to me that Jasmine was the sort of modern woman who disliked having to swallow come, whatever the circumstances or the relationship level she had reached with a particular man. Anal sex was an acceptable taboo. But not swallowing. Just not the right thing to do for educated women like Jasmine....

She leaves the office, and I'm left with my computer screen.

If only they were aware of my disgusting thoughts, I wouldn't have any staff left or any respect afforded me. The boss from hell. Just wouldn't do. But I have principles: I would never mix business with pleasure. Too complicated, despite the daily temptations. And we don't usually have a Christmas party anyway where we let our hair down. Not that I'm into drunken broom-closet sex or hanky-panky across the photocopying machine. A rule I invariably stick to, despite the genuine opportunities. It's easier to satisfy my vices and compulsions away from home ground. Should one of them leave, I might hit on her later under pretext of renewing acquaintance and solicitously inquiring how she is getting on with her new job elsewhere. It's worked before, I dare say.

I walk to the door, shout out to the girls working there that

I have a private call coming through and close the door to my office.

Back behind my desk, my cock is still part tumescent from memories of the spectacle of Jasmine with glasses on spreading her ass cheeks apart and readying her already moist aperture for the girth of my penis. I highlight my favorites on the browser menu and select a website:

Fetish.

BDSM.

Extreme.

I make a selection, and in the private cocoon of my office I begin masturbating to the images lining up on the screen.

The girls are safe.

For now.

CASUAL FRIDAY

Jolene Hui

Ice cubes. I could hear them rattling in the kitchen. I was sprawled out, naked, legs spread in the living room. Roger was fiddling around. I loved his tongue. He could eat my pussy for at least an hour straight. I'd stare at the clock above his mantel and try not to writhe around too much. After he was done, he'd come all over my tits.

My eyes were closed, but I knew exactly where my beer was located. I reached for it, kept my eyes closed, tilted my head up, and took a drink. It was humid in his penthouse on the bay. My skin was sweaty from rolling around on his white carpet for two hours. We had been fondling, kissing, and grabbing. I was only a little buzzed, and I think he was, too. I could never be sure with Roger.

"Keep your eyes closed."

"I am!"

"Keep it down. The neighbors." He kept rattling around. The ice cubes fell lightly into a glass bowl. "You really need to work on the yelling."

"Don't you like it when I'm loud?"

"I do. But my eighty-year-old neighbors do not."

My eyes were still closed. I turned my head toward him. The air from the freezer floated toward my face. He slammed the door shut.

"I hope your eyes are still closed, little missy." I could feel the wetness from my pussy dripping onto the carpet. He would be there shortly to lap it up again. I reached for my beer, but he grabbed hold of my ankles and dragged me about a foot across the carpet before I could get to the bottle.

I admit that I was not completely immersed in what Roger was doing to me. I was thinking about the man I wanted to screw so badly my ass hurt. Friday the thirteenth was coming up in two days, and I wanted to make him the thirteenth man I'd ever been with. A kinky and dark day for a kinky and dark encounter. I opened my eyes to see Roger's blond hair moving above my crotch. His hair smelled like floral shampoo.

Roger was a clean-cut boy: young, in his mid-twenties, and extremely athletic. He played tennis daily at the courts below his condo. He ran and lifted weights three times a week. His body was hard and inviting.

I tried to focus, but thoughts of my Friday-the-thirteenth man kept flashing through my mind. He was a vice president at the company where I worked, and his office was right down the hall from mine. He was good-looking, and he had money, but there was a slight problem with my thirteenth man. I couldn't tell if he was into me. I'd walk by in short skirts and high heels, and he never really reacted. Every once in a while, I'd pop my head into his office to talk to him, and he'd look over at me with his dark eyes and smile. He'd say a few cordial words, and I'd melt against his doorframe. I wanted his power and his looks, his hot cock in my pussy. I wanted to tear off his suit. Let him tie me up with his tie and belt....

"Oh, baby, I'm gonna come," Roger was straddling my chest and jerking his cock. "Touch your tits, baby. Touch your tits." I flashed back into reality. I wasn't sure if he had rubbed ice all over me. My thighs were cold, but I didn't recall him even touching me.

I looked at the ceiling as he came on my chest.

Where had I put my favorite black skirt?

The office was busy the next day. I opted to wear spiked heels with my short black skirt. No nylons for me. I wanted to show as much flesh as possible. Mr. Friday the Thirteenth walked in while I was making copies at the machine near his office. I stood up straighter and jutted my chest out. I was wearing a sleeveless white shimmery shirt that clung in just the right places. I turned toward him and smiled.

"Hey, Mark."

His eyes moved to my chest. My heart started to beat faster.

"Couldn't be better." He met my eyes again.

The rest of the afternoon, I sat at my desk and failed to do the most mundane tasks as I pictured us on the copy machine. His hands riding up my skirt, mouth on my neck. I rubbed a little bit on my chair. I could get off and no one would ever know. I stopped. I could feel myself flushing and I didn't want to get my chair moist. But then again, maybe I should have. Maybe the pheromones would have attracted Mark to me. I was convinced that I had to be giving off strong pheromones. I was excited every time I was around him.

When would Friday come?

That night at Roger's I was on my stomach on the floor. Roger had my ass cheeks parted and was licking slowly up my crack.

My hands were under my chin. I could see pieces of lint in his carpet. I closed my eyes and tried to enjoy the experience. Roger was an expert ass-licker. He really did have a knack for doing things with his tongue. I started wiggling my thighs. He's already eaten my pussy for an hour. My juices were all over his carpet, but I knew I was going to come again from his rim job. His tongue teased around the edge. Then he spread me wider and plunged his tongue inside me. I squealed as he licked and plunged until my cunt contracted again. I put my face on the carpet and breathed, lost once more in thoughts of Mark. Would he rim me? Or would he want my tongue in *his* ass? Roger stuck his fingers in my pussy with one hand and jerked off with the other. I felt his come hit my back as I imagined Mark fucking me against his desk.

"Could you take care of my plants this weekend?" Roger asked me when I was getting dressed.

I wasn't even aware he *had* plants.

He put his keys in my hand. "Just water the plants Friday and Saturday. I'll be back on Sunday, so you don't have to worry about that day."

"Where are you going?"

"To see my parents. I'll call you when I get back." He leaned over and kissed my cheek.

I left with a puzzled look. I was irritated that he had randomly asked me to water his plants. Why would I water his fucking plants? Who was I to water his plants? Most of the time I felt like I was doing him a favor by letting him eat me and then watching or listening to him jerk off. I wanted hard cock. I smacked the steering wheel with my hands. Roger's keys dug into my pocket.

Casual Fridays meant jeans, and I was sure to wear my most expensive and tightest pair. Every step I took in the form-fitting denim made me ache for Mark's cock. Mark was in his office. His dark hair was messy and he wasn't wearing a suit, but he still looked slick as hell. The blue button-up shirt was pressed but not *too* pressed. I stood in his doorway. He turned around and looked me up and down.

"Do you need anything?" I asked him.

He opened his mouth to say something and then closed it again. My black sweater was transparent if you looked close enough. Mark was staring.

I took another step into his office, then closed the door behind me.

"What are you doing tonight?" He fiddled with his fingers.

I was temporarily speechless. I studied his face. "Nothing planned, why?" As I had been doing for days, I pictured Mark's cock inside of me.

"Do you want to have dinner?"

"Of course." I couldn't believe he had asked me.

"I'll pick you up at eight."

I looked into his dark-brown eyes. Then I walked toward his desk. I smiled at him as I wrote down Roger's address on a Post-it. I had to water his plants anyway, and his penthouse was the perfect place for Mark to pick me up. I made sure to shake my ass as I left his office.

I touched myself in Roger's shower. I was slick under the water. The folds of my pussy were ready for a cock. I inserted a finger and played with my clit with the other hand. I breathed in the steamy air but was interrupted when the doorbell rang. "Fuck," I said, quickly turning off the shower and grabbing a white towel. I wrapped it around me and without thinking, ran to the door, dripping wet.

Mark's mouth dropped open.

I stood there in a towel with sopping wet hair. "Sorry, I'm not ready." I glanced at the clock and it was 7:30. I knew I hadn't misread the time. He was anxious. "Let me…"

"I'm early."

He was dressed in jeans and a black button-up with gray pinstripes. His black glasses frames were shiny in the penthouse light.

"I won't take long." I could feel his eyes on me as I walked to the bedroom. The bedroom was open with huge windows and a balcony. It connected to the living room where Mark was standing. I dried off near the window. It wasn't dark and, almost perfectly, the sun was setting. I didn't think I could make it to the dress, and I was right. I dropped my towel, my hair still wet, and walked to the arch between the living room and the bedroom.

Mark was on me almost immediately. His hands grabbed me all over, touching my breasts, then sliding down my body and grabbing my lower back, my ass, and my thighs. I undid his belt and felt him, hard, underneath his silk boxers. I got to my knees and put his cock in my mouth, keeping one had on the shaft and one hand on his thighs.

"Oh, baby, yeah," he said, his hands in my wet hair. I sucked him delicately, then a little more firmly while stroking his smooth penis. I didn't get too far. He grabbed me by the shoulders, turned me around, and I dropped down on all fours. His wet fingers were in my pussy. I arched my back.

"Mark," I moaned. I heard him tearing open a condom wrapper. He took his fingers out of me. I looked back to see him rolling the condom on. His cock was in my pussy quickly. I screamed. Roger wasn't there to scold me for bothering the neighbors, and I didn't care anyway. He rammed me furiously, but I had been wet for him for so many months there was no way he could chafe me. He grabbed my hips. The heels of my hands dug into the carpet. I looked out the windows to see the sun going down. The balcony looked so welcoming. I wanted him to bend me over the railing.

"Wait," I said. I walked over the door and opened it.

"But it's still light outside." He was worried that people might see.

"Just fuck me," I insisted, backing into him like an animal in heat. I grabbed the railing and stuck out my ass. Mark was just the right size for me and hard as hell. His hands were around my waist. I started to moan and wiggle against him. When I turned to the right, I saw the line of decks attached to the neighboring penthouses. I closed my eyes. I didn't care. Sure, I was in someone else's home fucking outside when it was still daylight, but it didn't faze me.

When he stuck his finger in my asshole, it was all over. I screamed in pleasure and came all over him. I felt him climax even though he was wearing a condom. He moaned. My eyes were still closed. He thrust a little bit more. I heard a gasp. My eyes opened. To the right, the old neighbors gawked at us with horrified looks on their faces.

"Who are you?" one of them thought to ask.

Mark had already run inside.

I didn't even know what to say. I turned to my left to see a man looking right at me.

Mark's clothes were already almost all back on when I got inside. I locked the door.

"Do you even live here?" he asked.

"Well, no, not exactly."

"What do you mean, 'not exactly'?"

"It's my friend's place." I was embarrassed for the first time ever in the penthouse.

"Why did you have me pick you up here?"

I couldn't think of anything clever to say. "I'm watering his plants."

Mark adjusted his glasses and buckled his belt. There was no way I could have stopped him as he headed out the door.

As my luck had it on that Friday the thirteenth, a bad situation got worse. Roger walked through the door as Mark breezed past. Apparently, his trip had been cut short.

"What the fuck is going on?" asked Roger.

I ran to the bedroom and threw on the dress. Roger followed me.

"I said, '*What the fuck is going on?*' "

I tossed his keys at him. "It really isn't my lucky day."

Roger didn't even have to tell me never to come back again. The penthouse was already a memory. I got in my car and drove as fast as I could, not looking back. I was sick of his rim jobs anyway. And I wouldn't mind a career change.

STRICT MANAGEMENT

T.C. Calligari

Fernando had no time for games. His meeting was in half an hour, and he had to change and get halfway across the city. These old hotels were quaint and beautiful but sometimes did not have the fastest elevators. He waited in front of the elevator doors laid out in an Art Nouveau pattern of ornate curves and swirls of brass. The hotel was not only an exemplary piece of the era, but the staff seemed to match the décor: upright, formal, polite but not too personal.

The brass arrow on the semicircular dial slowly crept toward the 1. Then the doors opened—first the inner solid-oak panels, and then the brass cage, pulled back by a dark-haired man wearing a small cap and a crisp blue uniform. He smiled and said, "Hiya. One moment"—and then ran out of the elevator, leaving Fernando gaping after him.

Where the hell had he gone? Fernando had no time to lose. He had to change clothes and make some notes for his speech on linguistics, plus get to the luncheon on time. In the elevator, he stared at the old push buttons and debated closing the cage doors. But would that be against hotel policy? Tapping his foot, he ran over his notes on neurolinguistic programming and waited, glancing at his watch every few seconds. He was conscious of the sweat stains on his shirt. A crisp suit was called for when he lectured. Had to look professional, had to be in control.

Finally, the elevator operator returned, smiling, barely moving faster than a stroll. Fernando bit back a retort but said: "I have to be at a lecture in a half-hour. Seventh floor, please."

"No problem," said the operator, closing the doors and whistling his way up to the seventh floor.

It grated on Fernando's nerves, but right now, everything did. If the lecture went well, there was a possibility of tenure at the University of Milan. But would he want to live in Italy? Admittedly, the food and wine were good, but there was something to be said for the cooler climes of the Pacific Northwest. Seattle had always appealed to Fernando's tastes. Cosmopolitan, he would call it, like him. But classy conservative is what his friends called him.

Maybe Italy was exactly what he needed. It could be good for a year, at least, and then there would be more choice of jobs in the U.S. The interview for the position was tomorrow, but he knew there would be important people in attendance at the lecture and it was essential to present well on all fronts.

They stopped on the seventh floor, and the operator eased the doors open. "See ya later," he called as Fernando walked away. Fernando shook his head and went to change, which he managed, along with some rewriting, in fifteen minutes. That left twenty-five to get to the hall—extra time for any traffic snarls.

He walked down the plush red-carpeted hall to the elevator and pushed the call button, then realized the elevator was open. But the operator was not waiting. Fernando peeked into the warm brown and red interior. No one. He looked left and right, and then spied the elevator operator chatting with a chambermaid at the far end. He stared at them, presuming the operator was aware of his charge waiting. Nothing happened.

Finally, Fernando called out, "Hello!" But the operator ignored him. He strode down the hall and called louder. "I have a lecture to get to. Can you take me to the lobby now?"

The operator looked at him. "Oh, yeah. Sorry." Then he chatted to the girl for another minute, until Fernando barked, "Now!"

Fernando tried not to grit his teeth. There was no hurrying this guy. He sauntered back to the elevator and took Fernando down.

"See ya," he called nonchalantly as Fernando hurried out to the waiting taxi. With the delayed departure and one traffic jam, he barely made it on time. He had to frantically grab his notes out of his case as he ascended the steps to the stage.

The first few minutes were rough, but Fernando found his pace and the rest of the lecture went well. He left feeling a bit more relaxed. It would be nice to drink a bit of wine to celebrate, but he had his regimen. Back to the hotel, an hour or two to study and formulate possible scenarios for the interview, then a light dinner. After, he would work out in his room—some sit-ups and push-ups—and then to bed early. The interview was at nine the next morning.

When he reached the hotel, he went to the front desk to collect messages. A young woman with black hair cut in a short pageboy, and wearing a smart suit in black with a cream-colored blouse buttoned to the neck, stood behind the desk. A brass pin denoted her position as manager, with a last name below that: BRAZALLOTTO. She smiled, and Fernando could see the beauty in her full lips and large, deep brown eyes. He glanced at the swell of her breasts beneath the conservative suit jacket and for a moment tried to envision her naked.

"There are no messages for you, Mr. Romero. How is everything so far?"

He hesitated, thinking of the slack elevator operator, but it didn't seem enough to complain about.

"Please, sir. If there is any problem, do tell us. We aim to keep this establishment a five-star hotel, which it has been for a hundred years. If anything is not to your liking, we will do our best to change it."

He drummed his fingers on the counter. "Well, it is not a big thing, but your elevator operator could be more prompt. I was almost late for my lecture today because he dallied here and there."

Her eyebrow rose and she seemed to stand straighter. "Oh, really? Please come with me." She stepped out from behind the desk, and Fernando was pleased to see her skirt was slim and tight, showing some calf and her black stiletto shoes. If he stayed in Milan, maybe he would look her up, once he was no longer a customer.

She walked to the elevator and pushed the call button. Glancing at her watch, she then looked at the brass plate and watched the arrow slowly swing around to the first floor. Then she looked at her watch again. The doors slid open and the elevator operator glanced at her from the corner of his eye and just nodded.

Fernando hesitated, then entered after the manager.

"Seventh floor, correct?" the operator asked.

Fernando just nodded. The manager said nothing but stood next to the back wall. They had nearly reached the seventh floor when she suddenly stepped forward and pushed the emergency stop button. The elevator eased to a halt.

The operator turned to her, looking uneasy. Fernando thought it very strange. Why had she ridden in the elevator with him? To see if the operator behaved? But of course he would before his superior.

"Mr. LaSalle, there has been a complaint about your inattentiveness. Mr. Romero here nearly missed his meeting today. You have been warned once already. Now you have a choice: to accept the punishment I deem fit for your misbehavior or to leave and find employment elsewhere."

LaSalle looked back and forth from Fernando to the manager. She did not look mad but she did seem resolute. "Uh, I'll...I'll take the punishment."

"Drop your pants and face the wall, please."

LaSalle's eyes widened. "What?"

"Your choice," was all she said, but a small glint fired in her eyes.

Fernando began to protest. "Look, Ms. Brazallotto, it's all right—"

"Please, Mr. Romero," she held up her hand. The nails were long and red, like her lips. "We believe in old-fashioned quality here and have a strict management policy. It has kept our hotel among the best for so long. The punishment must fit the deed and our promise."

Fernando shut up and looked down. LaSalle stared for a moment, his throat convulsively swallowing.

"Mr. LaSalle?"

His cheeks coloring, LaSalle turned to the side wall, then undid his pants and dropped them. The manager said, "Your underwear, too."

LaSalle jerked, breathing fast, and dropped his pants.

"Bend over and place your hands against the wall."

Tight-lipped, LaSalle bent over, his creamy asscheeks shining in the elevator's soft light. Fernando felt distinctly uncomfortable, but there was no way to leave the elevator. The manager stood in front of the doors, facing Fernando, with LaSalle's ass between them. She looked at Fernando once, and then raised her hand, her ruby-tipped nails glinting.

Her hand came down with a loud smack on LaSalle's left buttcheek. Both he and Fernando jumped, more at the sound than at the force of the smack. With feet braced apart and bending slightly from the waist, she laid another hand sharply upon his other cheek. Then she let fly five more slaps, all fast and fairly light. Pausing for a moment, she brought her hand far back and whaled into LaSalle's left cheek again. He grunted but muffled it. Her hand rubbed his cheek for a moment before she lifted and slapped twice more.

Fernando was riveted. He could not look away. He had never been spanked as a child. In fact, he had never seen anyone spanked before. But he was becoming embarrassingly aroused, though he'd never looked at men in his life. As his cocked press tighter against his suit pants, the manager continued to whale on LaSalle's buttcheeks.

LaSalle began to moan, and Fernando, feeling overly warm and very aroused, noticed LaSalle's cock perking toward erection, too. Somehow, that made him even harder. He shifted his hands, holding the briefcase in front. Glancing at the manager as she stopped to rub LaSalle's buttcheeks, and seeing her lithe form remain so calm and sensual at the same time, almost made him come. He bit his lip, sweat springing to his brow. He couldn't let go like this. Too shameful.

The manager patted lightly for a couple of seconds. LaSalle whimpered. Then she smacked his ass as hard as she could, pulling back each time to put force behind it and bringing his ass to a bright rosy glow. She stopped suddenly and, just once, ran her fingers along the underside of LaSalle's cock, over his balls, and across his anus.

It was too much for him and he came, jerking, splashing spunk against the dark wood walls, moaning and crying all at once as his buttocks tightened.

Fernando had to look away, closing his eyes, afraid that he too would come. Then the manager pressed the button and took them to the seventh floor. She opened the doors for Fernando.

"I trust that this should suffice for now, Mr. Romero. Call if you need anything." She turned back to LaSalle. "Clean up your mess and be at work on time tomorrow. You have the rest of the evening off." She got out of the elevator and, as if nothing had happened, sedately walked the length of the hall to the exit stairwell.

Stunned, Fernando staggered to his room. What *had* just happened?

He poured a glass of wine and drank it down, loosening his tie. He threw his jacket on the bed, then went and splashed water on his face. It was time to get down to rehearsing the interview, but the scene kept playing over and over in his mind. He couldn't concentrate and, though he started to fumble with his zipper, he couldn't bring himself to masturbate, either.

Fernando paced to the window, pulling back the curtain and looking out. Then he turned, poured another glass of wine, and made a pretense of spreading out his interview notes, all the while ignoring the tight tenting of his pants. A half-hour of abortive attempts to concentrate went by. The shock was just too much. How could anyone do something like that in a modern hotel and get away with it? How could anyone discipline employees like that? It would never happen in the U.S. Distracted, Fernando turned with the wine in his hand and knocked the bottle to the floor.

He could only stare as the wine splashed onto the pale carpet. Taking a slow sip from his glass, he reflected that he'd always been too wound up, too conservative, afraid of messing up, of being late. None of Fernando's friends had ever worried about time like him and they still had their jobs.

Turning back, Fernando picked up the hotel phone. He hesitated for a moment, feeling his erect cock throb. Then he dialed the front desk.

When a feminine voice answered, Fernando said, "Ms. Brazallotto, there is a problem I'd like to show you. No, it will not wait, as the damage will only spread. Yes. Thank you." Slowly, he hung up and then just stared at the phone, sipping his wine.

When a short sharp rap sounded on the door, he started. Fernando bit his lip. He could still back out, but instead he walked to the door and opened it. He turned back into the room before the manager could see his erection. Pointing to the spilled wine, he said, "I'm afraid I've been careless and let the wine spill."

After a moment's silence, she said: "It's just a spill. I will get the chambermaid to clean it up."

Fernando gulped the rest of his wine, to fortify his nerve, and then threw his glass against the bottle, breaking it. For good measure, he knocked a lamp off the table, too. "I seem to be out of control tonight."

When he looked at the manager, she stood there with her arms crossed and her carmine lips pressed closely together. "I see. Mr. Romero, we also have a strict policy about willful damage to hotel property."

His cock twitched under her withering gaze and he looked down.

"Drop your pants and underwear and brace yourself against the table."

Swallowing, Fernando did as he was told, never having heard sweeter words.

LUNCH MEETING

Marie Sudac

I show up at your office just in time for lunch. I know I shouldn't, but I sneaked a look at your datebook and saw that you don't have anything planned for today at noon. The receptionist is on the phone; she recognizes me and waves me in. Everyone in the offices surrounding yours has already slipped out for lunch. I find you in your office on the phone, talking about some contract or something. I close the door, pull the blinds, and look at you.

You register surprise as I pull up my short, businesslike skirt. I'm not wearing any panties, just a pair of thigh-high black stockings with lace tops that hook to my garters. I've shaved for you.

I pull my skirt back down and walk around the side of your desk as you say, "Okay, tell him to add the reversion clause." I'm down on my knees in an instant, and I have your pants open before you can say: "Mike, I'll have to call you back. I'm late for a lunch meeting." By the time I hear the phone hit its cradle, I've got your cock in my mouth. My lips slide up and down your shaft, and I press forward until the head touches the back of my throat. You're moaning softly, your hands going through my hair. I suck your cock until you're good and hard, and then I look up at you and see in your fiery eyes how much you want me.

I pull my skirt back up and climb into your lap, facing you. I guide your cock, sticky with my spit, between my lips. As I sink down on you, I'm a little surprised at how wet I am, at how good this feels. I knew I'd be turned on, but I swear I could almost come as the thick head of your cock presses against the walls of my pussy. I lean forward and kiss you on the lips, my tongue teasing yours as you moan. Then I start to fuck myself up and down on top of you, unbuttoning my shirt to free my breasts in their tight push-up bra. I pop one breast out of its cup and guide the hard nipple to your mouth; you start to suck as I continue grinding my hips up and down on top of you, pushing your cock into me.

You lean over, reach out, and draw your arm across your desk, sweeping everything violently to the floor. To my delight, you pick me up in your arms and push me onto the desk, my ass right at the edge and my legs still spread around you. The desk is the perfect height for you to fuck me, which you do with increasing enthusiasm as you lean forward to suckle my breasts. Your cock pounds into me, and I know I'm going to come soon, but you're not finished with me yet.

You pull out of me, ease me down off the desk, and turn me around. I'm like a doll in your hands as you force me over the edge of the desk, pushing me down so I have to spread my legs. Then you enter me from behind and reach under to press my clit as you start to fuck me.

I have to bite my lip to keep from moaning loudly. You're working my clit and fucking me, and I know I'm going to come any instant. I grab your hand and bite the palm to gag myself, bringing a whimper from your lips as I come in a muffled groan. My muscles clench around your shaft with each thrust, my orgasm overwhelming me as I bite on your palm. Then you're wrenching your hand from my grasp so you can grab my hips, holding me in the right position. You start to fuck me hard, fast, ready to bring yourself off inside me. "Please," I whimper. "Come inside me." I feel your thrusts getting faster and faster, and then you're exploding deep inside me, shooting your come into my pussy as I force myself back onto you, meeting your thrusts with my own.

When you're finished, you tug your cock out of me and I turn around, pushing you into your chair so I can get down on my knees and lick you before your cock softens all the way. The taste of your come and my pussy excites me still more, making my nipples stiffen. They're still moist from your mouth and feel cold in the air-conditioned office air. I lick you clean and tuck your cock back into your pants, zip you up, and buckle your belt. Then I stand up and pull down my skirt, keeping my thighs pressed tightly together in a largely vain attempt to keep from leaking on your office carpet.

I lean forward and kiss you once on the lips.

"Hope it was a useless lunch meeting," I whisper.

"We did some excellent work."

"We'll have to schedule them more often," I say.

"I like them unscheduled," you answer, as you smirk up at me.

I walk out past the receptionist, feeling the slickness of my pussy. People drift past me, returning from lunch. But I'm quite sure their lunch meetings weren't nearly as productive as ours.

SECRETARY'S DAY

Rachel Kramer Bussel

The day of my interview with one of the top law firms in New York City, I'm sweating through my brand-new designer suit, desperately mopping at my brow as I try to look composed. I'm fresh out of Rutgers, making my way through round after round of Manhattan office buildings, steep high-rises filled with bankers, lawyers, editors, and businessmen. Being a male applying for a job as an administrative assistant in the year 2007 is no easy task, let me tell you. Sure, we've said that we're all about equal opportunity, but to the minds of most bosses, the job is still that of a secretary, and she should be wearing a suit, heels, and pearls. I've done plenty of temp work, can type one hundred words per minute, and am prompt and efficient, not to mention having edited the school paper, but so-so grades and a major in American studies have landed me here today.

Well, that and the fact that women in suits make my cock hard. Unbearably hard. So hard it's almost painful. Women with power, the power to tower over me, to snap their fingers and make me obey—women who need their phones answered, need coffee brought to them, need a man "ready for anything," as the classic David Allen business book advises. The kind of woman who's got so much going on, who's turbocharged and needs someone to keep her action-packed, meeting-filled day running smoothly—those are the ones I dream about.

I've never told anyone about these fantasies, but I've had them for as long as I can remember. While my buddies went for the hot cheerleader types or the sweet girls next door, I was after the valedictorian, Audrey Hayden (and occasionally fantasized about our very prim and proper English teacher, who was actually British). With Audrey, I loved the way she raised her hand so knowingly in class, the smug look on her face when she finished a test, and, most especially, seeing her in her interview suits. She looked so efficient, so strong, as if she could take over the world, become president or an ambassador. Power wasn't something she questioned but something she owned, and rather than wanting power of my own, I wanted her power unleashed on me. With Audrey, I never got up the courage to tell her how I felt; I just looked longingly at her from afar.

My fetish aside, the fact is, if I want to move out of my parents' house in Hackensack, I need to get a job fast. I've been grilled about my background, ambitions, and educational history, usually by creaky older guys who look like they could barely get it up in the sack, let alone submit to a woman if they were smart enough to know how exciting it would be. Or could be, I guess I should say, since I've never actually realized these fantasies. I'm just starting to drift off into my go-to jerk-off material, where I'm down on all fours getting my ass inspected by a woman with sharp, spiky heels, bright red lipstick, and a voice that could cut glass, when I hear my name called…by a woman who looks like she's walked straight out of my naughty daydreams.

"Matthew Brick!" she calls, my name ringing out among the other, all-female, applicants. I stand up uncertainly; I definitely arrived after a few of the women here, and we all signed in on a clipboard. Some of them sigh, chomp their gum, blow their bangs huffily off their foreheads. They've noticed this preferential treatment, too. But I look up at the woman with gleaming black hair done up in a bun, wire-rim glasses, an off-white blouse, navy skirt, bare legs, and four-inch heels, and follow her, doing my best to look professional. "I'm Ms. Davis," she says, and something about the way she introduces herself—the inscrutable *Ms.*, the lack of a first name, the clipped tone— further sets me off. "I'm the senior partner here and in charge of overseeing the office, so this position will require a lot from whoever gets it. I expect my assistant to be at my beck and call pretty much twenty-four hours a day. You'll have a BlackBerry and cell phone, and I expect you to keep them on at all times." She's talking like I already have the job, while I try to keep my eyes straight ahead instead of on her ass as we walk down a long hallway. But it's hard not to stare. It's even harder not to picture myself on my knees, wrists bound behind my back, while my tongue plays between those pert cheeks.

Actually, I'd do anything she wants: massage her feet, get her coffee, spend hours under her desk tonguing her to orgasm. I'd even sit meekly, as I am now, while she flicks through papers on her desk. "I see here that you were the editor of your campus newspaper. Interesting. I'm curious how such a promising young man is now up for a position like this." She puts my résumé down and leans across the desk, her ferocious gaze gobbling me up. Something in her brown eyes sears into me, and I think of a cat opening its jaw, teeth flashing. "It seems to me that you'd want to be the one giving orders, not taking them, and I'm not sure how you'd feel about working for me. We're a big company, but I run things with an iron fist. Employees are expected to go above and beyond, and this position calls for it more than any other."

"Well, I got into some trouble in school, slacking off a bit, if you must know," I say, my heart pounding. "I was spending so much time running the newspaper that I let my studies get away from me. But I've changed my ways and am now ready to take on real, adult responsibilities." I don't tell her that my male professors had failed to inspire the kind of diligence, not to mention lust, that she already had done in me. There was no way I'd let someone like Ms. Davis down. "I'd be fully committed to making your day run smoothly." I don't add that I'd be fully committed to making her nights hum steadily along as well. I'm trying to quell my aching cock in my lap as I listen to her go through the duties that would be expected of me. It's much more than filing and answering phones. I'd be entrusted with an enormous amount of responsibility, would have to do errands for her at off hours, make phone calls, book trips, attend meetings, and make crucial decisions in her absence.

As she wraps up, I picture her sitting at her desk, while I stand behind her, massaging those majestic shoulders, helping to take away some of her cares. I tune back in to hear her saying, "I'll need some references from your old bosses, and I will confirm with you next week, but as long as you can prove yourself useful around here, you've got the job." She stands up and brusquely dismisses me, and I'm partly grateful because my arousal is too great to ignore. I'm tempted to use the bathroom in the building to jerk off, but I leave, walking by all those seemingly perfect girls. I feel their glares on my back as I wait for the elevator, then go to a nearby bookstore and relieve myself there, all the while thinking about being caught jerking off under my desk by Ms. Davis. I'm grateful that even though my grades weren't top

notch, my senior adviser and journalism professor, who'd over-
seen the campus paper, had adored me.

When I get the congratulatory call from Ms. Davis a few days
later, I'm ecstatic. "I'll see you first thing tomorrow, thank you
so much, I truly appreciate this opportunity—"

She cuts me off. "Enough with the gushing, Brick. Just show
up tomorrow and be ready to work." I do my best to get to sleep
early, knowing I'll have to take the bus in for a few more weeks
until I can find a nearby place of my own. I awake with the sun,
my cock hard, fresh from a dream in which Ms. Davis takes
her hair out of its bun and then lashes it across my face, then
tickles my cock with her long tresses before instructing me how
to wash, condition, and style it. I know none of the things I'm
fantasizing about are in my job description, but there's something about this powerful woman that makes me feel like she
might want to take things even further.

I arrive and do my best to put on a completely professional
appearance. I'm thrown right into the thick of things from the
first moment. Ms. Davis (whose first name is Vanessa, but I'm
never to call her that) barely has time to introduce me to anyone,
and I get lots of pitying looks from my new coworkers. "Hang
in there," is their common refrain, and I surmise that my prede-
cessor had only lasted a short while. Hints of her demise are
everywhere, but I'm too frantic answering Ms. Davis's inces-
santly ringing phone, organizing the incoming mail, and trying
to remember where things go and who's who that I don't have
time to ponder the desk's previous occupant too much.

Finally, a day of sweating and nerves and nonstop running
around (I ate a roast beef sandwich someone thrust on my desk
at one point in about three bites) comes to an end. I'm afraid
I'll get fired already for some imagined misdeed, but the office
quiets and everyone else goes home, so I eventually do, too. I'm

hoping for a special message from Ms. Davis, but she seems intent on whatever she's doing in her office, and I don't want to interrupt her. The rest of my first week follows pretty much the same routine, except that on Friday, just after six, I'm called into Ms. Davis's office. She summons me over the intercom, with the utmost formality, even though she could pretty much just yell from her office. I rise and walk slowly into her office, not wanting to let go of what promises to be a fabulous job.

"Sit down," she says, her voice severe. She looks me over, surveying every inch of my body until I want to shrink into the floor. Does she know about the lusty thoughts I've harbored? "I wanted to congratulate you on a successful first week. I know I threw a lot at you, and you handled it like a pro." My breath whooshes out of me with her praise. I'm not getting fired. Then her long nails tap sharply on her desk. "However, there are some additional duties of the job that I'm not quite sure you're capable of, so I called you in here to test them. These are duties of a more...*personal* nature," Ms. Davis says, her eyes drilling into me. I'm hard, and I wonder if she can tell. "Do you think you can handle these extracurricular tasks? Not every *man* is *up* for the job," she says, emphasizing my gender in a way that makes me squirm.

"Yes, Ms. Davis. I'm still available to you any time you need me. For anything," I finish, hoping I don't sound too impertinent. But apparently I don't, because then things take a turn for the surreal—and utterly arousing.

It's like she can see inside me with those penetrating gazes, because my new boss says, "Give me your tie, Matthew. I need it." This is the first time she's called me that, and I hope it means a shift in our relationship. Her voice is almost robotic, so stiff and formal, yet all the more seductive because of it. Part of me wants to be special to her—to be her boy toy, her trusted right-hand man, even her plaything—but an even greater part of me wants to be a speck of dust, replaceable, inconsequential, someone for her to truly use, abuse, and discard. I detect glimmers that I am the former but keep doubting them and assuming I'm the latter, and the mental seesaw has me permanently hard, wanting to please her and anger her all at once. When I don't move fast enough, she gets up, stands before me—towering over me, really—and tugs on the tie enough for it to choke me for a brief, beautiful moment. Then she turns, grabs a pair of scissors from her desk, and brusquely cuts it off me. "'For anything.' Those were your words, so I hope you'll remember them," she spits at me as she removes the tie from my neck. For some reason, I still feel tight there, almost choked, yet I'm perfectly free.

Ms. Davis is still standing over me, perusing me, as if deciding whether to kick me out or continue her delicious torment. She drills that gaze into me for a moment, then moves to her office door, shuts it, and locks it. She returns, then runs the dull edge of the scissors against my neck, making me flinch. "You're pathetic, you know that?" she says. "Well, I guess you do," she murmurs almost to herself when my dick pops right up at her comment. She raises one leg enough to show me a glimpse of her pale thigh, then gently trails the sharp heel of her shoe along my cock. Not enough to hurt, barely enough to make contact, but more than enough to let me know that she's the boss of me in every way that counts.

"On the floor," she says, pointing, as if there's no need for using any extra words with an underling like me. I do her bidding, settling on the gray carpet. I'm lying face up, practically inhaling tufts of carpet, dressed in a stiff, white shirt and perfect black pants, shoes shiny, while her dark-green alligator heel holds me down in the middle of my chest. She's simply resting her foot there at the moment, not pressing hard, but my heart is pounding as if she were bearing all her weight on me. I can just about see up her skirt if I move my head to the side, but when I make an attempt, she's having none of that. She has taken my mutilated tie and is swinging it in the air like a victory lasso.

"You've been waiting for this since that first day, haven't you? I don't need to be a genius to see what it's doing to you," she says, referring to the monster erection I'm sporting. Her foot moves down, slowly but menacingly, to my cock, then she runs the edge of her shoe along my dick. I wonder if she'll kick me there, or on my balls; if she'll stand on top of me with all her weight; if she'll take off her shoe and shove her stocking-covered smelly toes into my mouth. She does none of these things, though I'd have acquiesced to any.

"Take it out," she says, kicking the air near my zipper, depriving me of that most desired contact. Still, the chance to show her what I'm packing, to maybe make her day with my dick, is too precious to waste any more time. Under her gaze, I reach over the shoe she's placed back on my chest and unzip my pants, fumbling to unearth my hardness. Then I lie back while my hard-on rises straight up into the air. As turned on as I am being almost naked beside her, I can't help but want her to touch it.

"Very good. Now, we're going to go over some rules of the office to make sure you've been paying attention. Good help is hard to find and I'd rather have a virile man like you than one of those pesky, peroxide blondes who keep applying. And if you tell anyone I said that, I'll make sure you're sorry," she says.

I swallow hard, worried now only about coming spontaneously. "Now, what's the password to my computer?" As she fires off this question, Ms. Davis removes her sleek black jacket. I can see her breasts through her blouse; she hasn't worn a bra today, but you'd only know that without the jacket.

"Bitchgoddess-oh-seven," I immediately reply.

"How do I like my coffee?"

These questions are easy, but the look on her face tells me my job depends on getting them right. "Black."

"What kind of thread-count sheets must you request when I'm traveling for work?"

"Six hundred." My voice is getting more and more wobbly as she gets more and more naked. It's like I'm on a game show and each question I get right grants me another body part unveiled. Soon her breasts are only separated from me by the air, and the sight of her pert, pink nipples is enough to make me ache.

"How often do I need you to water my plants?" Hmm...this is a trick question, because she told me to water them a minimum of twice a day but preferably three. Two or three? Will I look like I'm showing off if I say three? The last two days I've been so busy, I've only done it twice, so I go with that.

"Wrong answer," she says, a cruel grin lighting up her face. "But you know what happens to boys who can't obey their bosses? They learn new ways to please them," she says. She steps over me so I can see her pussy. It's bare and pink and wet. I've only been with two other girls, and neither of them shaved, and both wanted to fuck with the lights out. Ms. Davis seems to want to view every inch of my aroused, terror-stricken body. Only the terror is quickly giving way to pleasure when I realize she is about to shut me up in the hottest way possible.

"Now, Matthew. This is really the only skill you need at this job. The girl who was here before you could barely find her own clit, let alone mine. She didn't know how to eat pussy or to make my ass happy. She didn't know much of anything, but she did let me spank her sweet bottom, so I let her stay for a while. Before her was a football player type who got a bit too aggressive, thinking that we'd take turns being in charge.

I want you to remember that I'm always in charge of you. I don't just need a secretary, I need a servant. A willing, devoted servant. You seem to fit the bill, but I want you to prove it," she continues, her voice commanding but, surprisingly, not cruel. Beneath her brusque words, I sense a tenderness, a capacity for giving that can only be revealed through this form of speaking. Not that I'm complaining; the way she's talking is only making me more aroused.

She surveys me one more time, and I must meet her approval because she gives me that same wicked, wonderful smile, then hikes up her skirt and lowers herself down so I'm enveloped by her pussy. It happens as if in slow motion, and soon we are no longer just secretary and boss, but owned and owner, man and mistress, servant and master. I relish not only the taste of her cunt as it meets my tongue, but also that she sees me as someone capable of absorbing her power and using my submission to strengthen her. Even though I'm young and perhaps idealistic, I know that she cannot seize power, cannot truly attain the levels of greatness she's capable of, in and out of the office, without an underling to support her. That is my job, and now, with my tongue, I do my best to excel at it. She makes it easy by pretty much shoving her sex into my mouth, by maneuvering all around, by using my face as her own personal Slip 'n Slide.

I moan against her cunt, feeling the vibrations reverberate from my lips to hers and back. I know I could get fired—hell, she could get fired—for doing this on company property, but I also have a feeling that anyone who tries to fire Ms. Davis would soon find himself in a similar position. Anyone would melt in front of her, and as she overtakes my mouth, I do feel as if I'm melting into the ground and into her. She's melting, too, softening bit by bit as her grip on my ears loosens and her moans get softer. Instead of yelling directions, she's moaning—not words, just sounds. Ms. Davis is turning into Vanessa, turning from corporate to climactic, and all because of me!

I try to memorize the taste and feel of her pussy lips, so different from the tentative lapping I've done before. With her positive feedback spurring me on, I chance to raise my hands and slide them around her legs so I can play with those lips, stroke that clit. She lets me play with her so that I'm feeling the wondrous sensual softness inside her. I was right—she does have a gentler side, and I'm touching it right now. Her face looks almost relaxed, younger, yet just as beautiful as before. She still controls me, which she proves by suddenly pressing my head to the floor with her palm and grinding away again. "Suck it!" she says, and I suck her clit, suck her lips, suck everything I can, wishing I had two or even three mouths to suck other parts of her as well.

Finally, after what feels like an hour but I later learn has only been fifteen minutes, she comes, her orgasm a rumbling, powerful wave crashing against my mouth, her body bouncing against me as she crests. She rises and looks remarkably composed for someone who's just had her pussy licked so intensely. I feel like we've just had sex on a fast-moving vehicle or a comet. My heart is pounding and I'm glad I'm lying down. I'm so dizzy with desire for her, I almost ignore my cock. This craving, this need, goes deeper than my dick. But Ms. Davis hasn't forgotten it. She smiles down at me, then goes to her desk and returns with a small bottle. I don't know what's in it, until she opens it and starts pouring the clear liquid directly onto my cock. It's cool and slippery and I moan. "Jerk yourself off. Give me a show. But don't come on my carpet," Ms. Davis instructs me. "Use this," she says, handing me a bunch of tissues.

I'd have thought it would be hard to masturbate in front of anyone else, let alone the woman of my dreams, who also happens to be my new boss, but it turns out to be surprisingly easy. I look up at her as she sits at her desk as if overseeing me. I don't worry about whether the style I use is what she wants, knowing she'll correct me if I'm doing anything wrong. Instead, I just focus on the extreme pleasure of being watched by her. In practically no time, I'm scrambling for the tissues as my orgasm bursts into them. She nods approvingly, though I'm suddenly shy. We've shared something so intimate, yet there is still a great distance between us. I remind myself we are not lovers or even friends but, rather, still secretary and boss. For a moment, I'm wistful and wish our positions were different so I could get even closer to her.

She walks over as I'm zipping my fly. "Very good, Matthew. I had a feeling about you when I saw you in the waiting room. Now, I have an early brunch tomorrow, but I'm going to need your assistance in the late afternoon. I have some…home office affairs to take care of. Filing, typing, foot massage, that type of thing. I'll expect you there at four." She doesn't ask if I'm free; she knows I'm the very opposite of free. I'm hers, pure and simple; even if she were to fire me, I'd do that kind of work for free.

"Oh, and dress casual. Very casual, as in no underwear. You won't be needing it." She dismisses me with another nod, and I go the bathroom to reluctantly wash my face of her juices before walking back to my desk to shut off my computer and grab my coat. As I sign out, the security guard peers closely at me, as if he can see or smell or simply sense who I am now. A secretary but also a slave. A bottom through and through. A devotee. I give him a big, dazzling smile. I don't really care what anyone else calls me, as long as Ms. Davis calls me hers. And while I know that the formal holiday of Secretary's Day (now renamed Administrative Professionals Day) takes place in April, I'm going

SECRETARY'S DAY   89

to celebrate mine as of now, in June, because, really, how lucky can a guy get? I've got a paying job and a boss who knows exactly how to whip me into shape, one who keeps me almost permanently hard, *and* who wants me to "work" weekends. My Wall Street friends can eat their hearts out. I'll be too busy eating Ms. Davis to notice.

ONE CUBICLE OVER

Jeremy Edwards

M indy made me sex-obsessed in a way I hadn't been since eighth grade.

Here I was, a well-adjusted, experienced man of thirty-two. Throughout my adult life I had studied with women, worked with women, socialized with women, seduced and been seduced by women, formed strong bonds with women, built complicated relationships with women, and had one-night stands with women. I had been fraternally friendly with them, professionally proper with them, uproariously ribald with them...and gloriously, so gloriously, intimate with them. I respected women, I admired women, I learned from women, I sympathized with women, I adored women.

In the course of all this, I'd experienced captivating sexual obsession—but always in the sophisticated manner of a man of the world. These were grown-up obsessions explored on moonlit beaches furnished with champagne, or in boutique hotel rooms with their inevitably inviting beds and bathtubs, or at 1:00 a.m. rooftop parties for two.

And suddenly one humdrum Tuesday, a woman whose face, though pleasant, I would never have picked out of a crowd... and whose interests had little or no overlap with my own...and whose personality, though undoubtedly agreeable, didn't really grab me...was assigned the cubicle next to mine. And just as suddenly, I became, for all practical purposes, a thirteen-year-old again.

It must have been pheromones, I kept telling myself. I must have been responding to her on an unconscious, olfactory-driven level that made my chemicals boil and my sexual intellect regress. No matter how blatantly I failed to connect with her, her femaleness screamed itself to me in a primal way.

Mindy is sitting in the cubicle next to mine. Mindy, who is female, is in the cubicle next to mine. Mindy, who has breasts and slender fingers and wears dresses and skirts, is in the cubicle next to mine. Mindy, who shaves her legs and whose underpants have no fly and who inserts fingers into herself to masturbate, is in the cubicle next to mine. Such were the endless, compulsive trains of thought that displaced my priorities as a skilled graphic designer facing a precarious stack of deadlines.

Meanwhile, Mindy had hair that was a color I thought of as "nondescript" and an hourglass figure that struck me as "predict-able" and a tone of voice that reminded me of my sister's. Her eyes glazed over on the few occasions I tried to talk to her about Art Nouveau or exotic beetles, while her rapturous discussion of car trends left me in neutral.

After I had somehow managed to complete the most urgent of my assignments with Mindy's chemicals simmering next door, I took a couple of personal days. I thought if I didn't go near her from Wednesday night until Monday morning, I might shake this obsession. But all I did from Wednesday night until

Monday morning—to the extent my body was up to it—was fondle and shake myself to absurd orgasms while thinking about how Mindy had a vagina and small feet and a hairless ass. The mind-set may have been eighth grade, but the orgasms were industrial strength. What was driving me? Could I somehow, unconsciously, smell her even from home? Ridiculous. Unless...

It was a natural conversation for me to start on Monday morning.

"How was your weekend?"

"Good, thanks," she replied. "Yours?"

"Long and absorbing," I answered truthfully. "I mostly just did things at home."

"Yeah, I was mostly home, too," she stated matter-of-factly.

This was the opening I'd wanted. "What neighborhood do you live in?"

"I have an apartment near the symphony. I've lived there about a year now."

Aha! But I realized there must be hundreds of apartments, in dozens of buildings "near the symphony." It would be audacious to assume that she lived in one of the few studios beside, above, or below mine that could plausibly be within smelling distance.

"Yep," she continued, "near the symphony." And then she tossed off the address. My address.

And yet if she'd been living in my immediate vicinity all this time, exuding her potent pheromones, then why had I never been affected by them before we became coworkers? Had sitting a mere cubicle away from her somehow triggered something— akin to an allergic reaction—which could now be rekindled by a weaker, more distant version of the same stimulus? For lack of a better theory, I accepted this premise that close exposure to Mindy's chemicals had made me hypersensitive to her.

"It's kind of funny that I ended up in that area," Mindy was saying, "since I'm totally uninterested in music—of any kind."

More evidence, of course, that we had nothing in common. I could not even imagine living without music. I appeared to be a thoroughly unsuitable match for Mindy.

Mindy, whose legs converge in a neat, feminine juncture instead of a collage of male genitalia like my own. Mindy, who has a smooth neck and a high voice and would sing soprano, if she didn't hate music. Mindy, who keeps her knees together when sitting on the bench in front of the elevator in our lobby. Mindy, who walks nonchalantly through a door marked WOMEN *when it's time to wash up for lunch.*

Mindy's computer crashed a minute later. "Argh!" she said from her cubicle. Argh. I wondered if she said "Ngh" when she approached orgasm. I had fucked three or four women in my time who said "Ngh" as they ramped up to climax, and I wanted desperately to know if Mindy said "Ngh."

Mindy couldn't have cared less about the food I liked or the authors I treasured. She loved camping and skiing, which I couldn't stand. She never laughed at my jokes. Nevertheless, I spent my first morning back at work pondering whether she said "Ngh" in bed.

We had two single-occupant, unisex bathrooms in our office. That afternoon, as I was heading for the restroom nearest our department, Mindy came out of it. I had heard her on the phone just a minute or two earlier, so she'd obviously just gone for a quick pee—or maybe simply to glance in the mirror.

As I closed the door, it became obvious that Mindy had indeed pulled her tight little jeans down in this room. The aroma of her femaleness was as overwhelming as it was immediate. No unconscious senses were required to detect her this time. Though my intention in sequestering myself here had been to take a piss,

I found myself stroking my cock as I stood at the toilet, gazing down on the seat that had hosted her bare ass moments before, her sex diffusing into the small room's atmosphere. *Mindy is female. She sits down to urinate and makes the bathroom smell like cunt. Her cunt.* In seconds, I was ejaculating into a palm full of bleach-white toilet paper.

Over the next few days, my sense of smell finally seduced my other senses. Now, I could not look at Mindy without admiring the subtle grace of her features; I could not listen to her talk without feeling tremors. How, I marveled, could I ever have found her bland and her voice ordinary? I began to see my previous unresponsiveness to her physical charms as a reflection on my own shortcomings.

Even more, her personality began to fascinate me. Her lack of interest in the things I cared about somehow became an *intriguing* lack of interest. Her enthusiasm over subjects that bored me became *enchanting* enthusiasm. I was infatuated with everything about this woman, even though I knew it was ultimately just the result of mischievous molecules from her vagina tickling my horny nose, day in and day out. I didn't care. I just wanted to fuck her all night, every night, and really get to know her during the intervening days.

On Friday, the day she wore the soft white jeans with the pocket buttons, I couldn't hold back any longer. You know the sort of pants I mean—with cute little button-down pockets on the ass, impractical as pockets but intoxicating as textures, ornamenting pert cheeks the way nipples ornament breasts. When Mindy was standing at the photocopier with her back to me, I found I could not take my eyes off those little buttons. All I wanted to do was unbutton each pocket in turn and caress her ass.

I had three deadline-sensitive projects on my desk. But the only projects I worked on that morning consisted of various fantasies that each involved (a) unbuttoning those pockets and (b) fondling Mindy's bottom through the thin layer of fabric inside them. (For the purposes of these fantasies, I took the liberty of presuming Mindy to be wearing a thong.) By lunchtime, I had already masturbated my head off in the john three times.

"Hey, do you have plans this weekend?" Any reservations I might once have had about asking this question were by now comfortably submerged beneath my consuming desire to touch Mindy's body.

She smiled. "I was going to ask you the same thing."

So dinner that night it was, at a restaurant near our building. It was a curry place—one of the few cuisines on which we agreed. It seemed appropriate that we were going somewhere enticingly fragrant.

"They don't serve alcohol," she warned me. Mindy liked beer; I liked wine.

"No worries," I ventured in reply. "I've got stuff at my place, so we can go up for a drink afterward."

"Perfect."

Dinner conversation involved a predictable assortment of dead ends. And yet there was a level of comfort there, a rapport. We had come a long way in two weeks of cubicle-bumping.

After dinner, we very naturally slid onto opposite ends of the convertible couch in my pad, drinks in hand. We raised our glasses in a casual, unspoken toast.

"You realize we have nothing in common," said Mindy after a sip of beer.

"Oh, yes," I replied.

"But you're cute," she stated, as if this were a fact. "That's why I wanted to go out to dinner with you...and everything." She blushed. I couldn't remember the last time I'd spent an evening with a woman who blushed. "How about you?"

"You mean, why did I want to go out to dinner—and every-thing?"

"Yes. Even though we—"

"I know, I know. Even though we have nothing in common." We laughed together, perhaps for the first time, united by a shared awareness of our irreconcilable differences.

Mindy's candor inspired my own. "Don't take this the wrong way, but—believe it or not—I wanted to go out with you because…" I hesitated and made a quick detour. "Now, I think you're cute, too, and I like you. I like you more with each moment, in fact." I cleared my throat. "But I really wanted to go out with you because…I can unconsciously smell your cunt all day long, and it's driving me wild."

Her mouth dropped open. Was it shock? Incredulity? I thought I saw her eyes tearing up.

"Wow," she said softly, her soprano pitch suddenly husky.

With great delicacy she placed her beer on the coffee table, next to my glass of wine.

Then she pounced on me, and I was enveloped in arms and legs and breath and liquid kisses, my head spinning in the strongest dose yet of Mindy's aroma. Of all the times I had fantasized about Mindy, it had never occurred to me that she might go even wilder than I would, that she would fling herself on me and fuck me like she'd been waiting for it all her life.

I don't remember how, or when, our clothes came off. But I'll never forget the way she rode me, her thighs trembling while she guided herself up and down my pole, juicing every ounce of plea-sure from the machine of our genitals. She smelled like home, like dinner, like laughter and dessert…and, of course, like cunt.

"Ngh," she said, her face a grimace of hard-earned bliss. "Ngh," she reiterated, and reiterated, with shorter and shorter interludes between iterations. When she'd taken us as high as we could go, I clutched her butt cheeks for my own ninety eternal seconds of free fall.

Afterward, she rolled into the crook of the loveseat. I dropped to the floor, preparing to make a proper meal of her. But her ass was facing out, and I couldn't ignore it. I had to kiss every inch of this ass—this ass I had once dismissed as "ordinary"—before going near her pussy, potent though the pussy's olfactory beckoning was.

When I had kissed cheeks and crack so comprehensively that Mindy's bottom was jiggling in my face like it had its own motor, I moved at last to the heart of the matter. Tonguing and kissing every possible place between her legs, I felt drunk on her essence. It was the oxygen my lungs had craved since I met her. And though Mindy claimed not to have a musical bone in her body, her soprano trills were tonally perfect every time she hit a climax. "Ngh" for fucking and trills for being eaten, I noted, having always been a devoted student of languages—unlike Mindy, who could rattle off sports stats but had flunked out of Spanish.

"I have to pee," she said after I'd finally exhausted her.

My couch smelled like Mindy's cunt. My body smelled like Mindy's cunt. My bathroom would soon smell like Mindy's cunt. And I knew I would do my best to make sure that Mindy returned again and again, so that her delicious scent could never dissipate and leave me deprived.

Mindy the delightful. Mindy the compelling and enchanting. Mindy, who, at that very moment, was making her splendid, fluid, utterly naked way toward my bathroom. Mindy, who was, and always would be…Mindy.

PERKS OF THE JOB

Kristina Wright

J enny, would you ask Edward to come by my office as soon as possible?" My words were clipped, almost sharp, but they made me clench my thighs together. "The sooner the better."

If I sounded at all eager, Jenny didn't let on. Her voice crackled over my intercom, "Sure, Victoria."

I sat there, waiting. It wasn't as if I didn't have work to do. I did. I simply was incapable of it at the moment. Interviews would wait. The stack of new-hire applications would wait. Everything, even my job as director of human resources of the largest accounting firm in North America, would wait until I was finished with Edward.

He arrived in less than ten minutes. He did not knock, he never did. It annoyed me, which was precisely why he never knocked.

"I heard you wanted to see me," he said, taking the chair across from my desk. He sat back, legs splayed in such a way as to draw my gaze to his crotch. The expensive fabric of his navy blue trousers was stretched taut across his sizable bulge. I squeezed my thighs tighter.

"Yes." I fumbled through the files on my desk, but the words were a blur in front of me. "You know performance evaluations are coming up in a month." He didn't respond. I looked at him, willing him to speak.

Finally, reluctantly, he said, "Yeah?"

"So why do I have ninety percent of everyone else's evaluations and none of yours?"

He yawned and gave a little stretch. I imagined his well-defined body beneath his tailored suit jacket and the cream-colored shirt under that and it made me wet.

"You'll get them, Vickie, right on time."

I hated the nickname Vickie, especially in the workplace. It sounded so...pedestrian. Which, of course, was why he used it. "I need them early so I can go over your notes and make changes."

"You won't need to change anything."

"I might."

His lip curled up in an insolent grin. "You won't. Besides, that isn't the reason you called me in here."

"It isn't?" I feigned ignorance as I restacked the files in front of me.

"No, it isn't. Is it?"

It was my turn to be silent. I didn't dare meet his gaze. Edward had worked for me—under me, as he liked to say—for two years. I had hired him to be the assistant director of human resources because I saw in him the same qualities I had, at least when it came to business. He was charming and good with people, which made him a fine candidate for the department. He also had what looked like an enormous dick, which made him a fine candidate for my bed. Of course, my company had a very strict policy against fraternization, which, ironically enough, I wrote. I might be ruthless, but I was ethical. So far, I hadn't let Edward into my bed. But I did let him into my office.

"Vickie?"

"What?" I stubbornly refused to look at him.

"You didn't call me in here to give me a hard time about the evaluations, did you?" His tone had changed. It was no longer frat boy insolence he exuded. It was something else, something more, something I was so strongly, powerfully drawn to that it made me risk everything for even a brief taste.

I shook my head.

"What?"

Hot tears pricked my eyes. I looked up, feeling the sting of humiliation like a blow. "I didn't call you in here to talk about performance evaluations," I said softly.

"So why did you call me in here?"

I hated him for making me say it. Hated that I would have to admit my weakness, even though he already knew it well. I looked him in the eye and said, "Because I need you."

I knew he wouldn't be satisfied with that answer, but I refused to give him more.

He sat up straighter. "Need me for what? To do some paperwork? To discuss an employee?"

I shook my head, eyes downcast once more.

"Why do you need me, Vickie?"

I hesitated a minute, two, five. The words were caught in my throat. I couldn't speak.

He stood up. "You're wasting my time," he said, his voice cold. "I have work to do, boss."

He practically snarled the word *boss*.

I looked up then, startled. "Please, wait. Edward, don't go." My voice was breathless, faint. I didn't recognize myself.

He stood there across from my desk, staring down at me. Slowly, deliberately, he said, "Then tell me why you need me here."

I couldn't say it, but I had to. I had to speak, or he would leave. I had to confess my sins, or he would abandon me. "I need to be punished," I blurted.

He rocked back on his heels, not from surprise but from pleasure. "Good girl," he said softly, his tone that of a benevolent parent. "I knew you could say it."

I didn't want to, but I couldn't help smiling under his gaze.

"Stand up," he snapped, and my smile faltered.

I hurried to do as he demanded, stumbling a bit as my heel snagged on the mat under my chair. I rested my hands lightly on the desk for balance, feeling suddenly lightheaded.

"Come over here."

I moved quickly around to the other side of the desk, careful not to touch him. My body practically hummed with anticipation and anxious, unfulfilled need. I stood in front of Edward, hands clenched in tight fists at my side, resisting the urge to lean into him. He was several inches taller than me, and the top of my head came only to his chin. I stared at that square, firm jaw line, so sexy and so unforgiving, willing him to speak. To give me what I needed.

"Are you wearing panties, Vickie?" he said softly, his breath a faint whisper across my forehead.

I nodded.

"Bad girl. Take them off."

I didn't hesitate and I didn't look at him as I fulfilled his request. I hiked my skirt up only so far as necessary to hook my thumbs in the sides of my panties and tug them down my legs. I balanced precariously, first on one leg, then the other, removing the hot pink wisp of silk and holding the panties out for him.

He took them, inspected them. Sniffed them. "They're damp," he said at last.

I could feel my cheeks flush hotly. "I'm sorry."

He chuckled, but it wasn't friendly. "Why are they wet, Vickie?"

I could have given him a coy answer and told him they were wet because he turned me on, but that wasn't what he wanted. I knew what he wanted. The game had only just begun, but I forfeited it with my next words. "Because I'm a naughty slut, sir."

"Yes, you are. And you need to be disciplined," he said. "Open your blouse."

With slow and clumsy fingers, I unbuttoned my blouse. It wasn't a difficult task, but his steady, scrutinizing gaze distracted me. Finally, my blouse hung open, revealing my pink, lacy bra that perfectly matched the panties Edward had tucked in his pocket.

"Pretty." He reached out as if to caress my breasts, but instead pinched each nipple through the fabric of my bra. When they stood up in tight, painful points, he smiled. "Better. Now, we don't have all day, so I suppose I'd better take care of the rest."

I stood like a mannequin while he prepared me for his pleasure. He tugged my blouse halfway down my arms, then pulled the shirttails back behind me, tying them in a knot so that my arms were pinned at my sides. I cringed over the wrinkles he was leaving in the fabric, but that thought fled when he tugged my bra down, freeing my breasts from the lacy cups. The feeling was uncomfortable, awkward, foreign. I would have preferred to be topless before him, but that would have been too easy on me. And Edward was never easy on me.

Next, he tugged my skirt up to my hips. The fabric was soft and clingy and it swathed my hips like a belly dancer's belt. There I stood, fully dressed but for my panties, with my breasts and pussy exposed. It was embarrassing. Humiliating. Exhilarating.

Edward stood back, admiring his handiwork. "Lovely. You are lovely, Vickie. Do you know that?"

"Thank you, sir," I murmured, eyes downcast. I could feel the wetness gathering between my legs. Without panties, I feared it would trickle down my thigh and betray my lust. Not that Edward didn't already know.

"Turn around and bend over," he ordered.

It was difficult, maneuvering with my arms pinned at my sides and my skirt around my hips, but I managed to turn and face the desk, bending at the waist. It was an awkward, uncomfortable position, but I bore my discomfort silently, staring at the mahogany surface of my desk.

Edward moved closer until he was standing beside me. He stroked my back, over the curve of my ass, stopping before he could touch my cunt. "Very nice," he murmured as he stroked me over and over, never quite touching me where I most desperately needed to be touched.

I felt myself arching against his hand like a cat in heat, aching for the warmth and strength of his hand, desperate to feel his fingers between my thighs. I should have known better than to let my guard down, but Edward was just that good. At the first whimper of pleasure, he reached under me, quick as a viper, and pinched and twisted my nipples viciously. I yelped and tried to stand upright, but his hand was on the small of my back, holding me down.

"Easy, little girl," he said. "Be good for me."

I whimpered as his hand slid down my back and hovered over my ass. I bit the inside of my cheek to keep from crying out as he paused. I imagined I could feel the stir of the air as his hand moved through it, then he slapped my ass with a sharp, stinging smack.

I yelped again and jumped a little, bumping against the desk.

"Be quiet, Vickie, or I'll be forced to gag you."

I remembered the time he had used my own panties to silence my cries, and I quickly clamped my mouth shut.

"Have you been a very bad girl, Vickie?"

"Sir?"

He stroked the indentation at the base of my spine. "If you were just a little bad, I'll give you a spanking with my hand." He slid his finger down, teasing the crease of my ass. "But if you've been truly naughty, I'll have to whip you with my belt."

I shivered. He could be ruthless with his hand, spanking me until my ass stung and I was sure his hand must be swollen and painful. But with his belt...he was brutal, the pain lingering for days, my ass almost too sore to allow me to sit.

I contemplated my choices. I mumbled softly at the desk, "I've been very, very bad, sir."

"Well, then, I guess it's the belt for you, little girl."

I heard the metallic sound of his belt buckle as he undid it, then the quick swoosh of leather on fabric as he pulled it through the loops. I stood there, bent over, my face inches above my desk, my legs braced for the blows to come, completely exposed to his view.

"Ask for it," he said.

I had already asked, but I knew better than to whine. "Please, Edward," I whispered. "I need to be punished."

"What do you need?" There was no emotion in his voice.

"I need to be whipped."

"Tell me what you did to deserve it."

I thought frantically. Earlier, I had compiled a list, but now all I could think about was the sting of the belt. "I—I don't know."

"Vickie." He said my name like a warning, and I didn't take it lightly.

"I reprimanded Jenny for being late Monday," I said quickly. "Then I came in twenty minutes late on Tuesday."

I heard the whoosh of the belt through the air even as I said the word *Tuesday*. It landed with a sharp crack squarely across my ass and, though I had expected it and knew how it would sting, it still made me jump and whimper.

"What else?"

"I lied about the performance evaluations. Only half of them have been turned in."

Edward chuckled. "Only half?"

"A third," I admitted.

He whipped me twice in quick succession, and I cried out.

"Careful, Vickie. You wouldn't want Jenny to hear you," Edward said. "Next?"

I took a deep breath, trying to stifle the urge to cry. Then I confessed my worst transgression. "I went through your work e-mail to see if you're dating anyone."

"You what?"

"I'm sorry," I whispered.

My confession earned me a frenzy of belt lashings. I squeezed my eyes shut and whimpered softly with each stroke of the belt. Edward whipped me with increasing force, changing directions so that the belt never hit me in the same place twice. My stomach muscles were exhausted from supporting my upper body at such an uncomfortable angle, so I bent a little more and rested my warm, damp cheek against the cool surface of my desk.

"Lazy girl," Edward said. He angled the belt up between my legs and landed a particularly wicked blow across my bare pussy, which caused me to moan and bite my lip, then raise my head from the desk.

"Better. You're learning."

On and on it went, slap after slap of the belt on my bare

ass and thighs, with the occasional smack on my pussy until I was a quivering mass of nerve endings begging for release. I was whimpering softly, or so I thought, until Edward ceased whipping me and pressed his erection against me. Even the soft fabric of his trousers felt like the roughest sandpaper on my sensitive, swollen ass.

"You're making enough noise to bring the entire staff running," he said.

His hands glided over my lower back and ass, stroking the marks he'd left. I knew I'd have red welts for at least a day or two. Perhaps longer. His touch didn't soothe; it wasn't meant to. He was examining his handiwork—and judging by the size of his cock nestled against me, he was very pleased with his art.

"What did you find in my e-mail?"

I swallowed hard. Being bent half-naked over my own desk and whipped into submission was not nearly as humiliating as having to admit I'd been snooping. "Nothing," I whispered.

Edward slid his hand down over my hot, tender ass and slipped two fingers into my dripping pussy. "What do you think that means?"

He fucked me gently, steadily, then slid a third finger inside me. I couldn't form the words to answer his question.

"Victoria?" He used his thumb to massage my asshole. "What does it mean that you didn't find anything?"

I knew it didn't really mean anything at all except that he didn't use his work e-mail for personal use, as per company policy. But I knew what he wanted to hear. "It means you're not seeing anyone."

His fingers kept up their steady rhythm in my cunt. "Good girl. Now why did you want to know?"

I gasped as he stroked my G-spot. "I just wanted to know."

His fingers stilled. "Why?"

I whimpered, pushing my pussy and ass back toward him. "Because I want this to be more."

"You do?" He fingers began moving again, harder, deeper. Driving me forward over my desk. I rested my head against my desk again, but he didn't reprimand me. "What about policy?" I couldn't breathe. I couldn't think. All I could do was come on his hand, my pussy clenching around his fingers. "Fuck policy," I moaned.

He stroked me gently as my body quivered against him. "Good girl. Good, good girl," he crooned.

"Thank you," I whispered, my head still on the desk. I whimpered softly as he withdrew his fingers from my wetness.

He helped me stand and untied my shirt so I could move my arms. He smiled as he watched me adjust my clothing, sans panties since they were still in his pocket. "You're an amazing woman."

I smiled, flushed with pleasure and sexual release. "Thanks. So my place around eight?"

His smile faded. "No."

"Oh," I said, as startled as I had been at the first strike of the belt.

"Your place—around seven."

"Oh!"

LONELY AT THE TOP

Savannah Stephens Smith

I fucked my way to the top.

Not many women admit that these days, if they ever did. But I'm sure, despite changes in how we look at men and women, work and power, that a lot of women—and maybe some men, too—still do it. You grab your chances any way you can, and what's offered up in return is old and compelling. And oh so hard to resist.

Maybe fewer have to do it these days. Times have changed, even in the business world. Me, I liked to fuck, and I had no commitments at home. I could have had. I'm not gorgeous, but I am just fine. But I was also a busy woman with a career that meant a lot to me. My job was my life. I didn't have much patience with nonsense, wasting time in boring bars, being coy with a straw, hunting for Mr. Right. *Mr. Right Now* would do. And my belief was that if a good lay was going to give me pleasure and get me ahead, I'd take that over Joe in the corner any time. If a shortcut's available, there's no point in driving all over the country to get to where you really want to be.

And I wanted to be at the top. Who doesn't?

Fucking. As a strategy, it's as old as time, and it seems as effective now as it was aeons ago when Oga found that putting out for Og got her a warmer spot by the fire and a little extra grilled saber-tooth, to boot. It's human, as human as we all are, and I won't apologize for it, even now.

Sex is something we all do, all want, except for priests and the hopeless. And we've seen what happens when men's desires are sublimated. They turn dark and twisted. It's not healthy to deny your lusts.

And we all have desires, sometimes buried, sometimes right out in the open. And one of my gifts is for knowing desire, for finding it, no matter how hidden. It's like holding a narrow, forked branch, taken from the earth, in your hands, then closing your eyes and just feeling the song in the ground and knowing that's where the water lies. And gentlemen, some of you run deep. And strange.

So there you have it, what you all suspected is true: I fucked my way to the top.

Of course, some of you know that already. Just as some of you know just how I liked my fun along the way. Some men are so grateful to get a bit, and to get it from a good-looking woman with a few brains in her head, too. For heaven's sake, some of you acted like you'd won the lottery, and all I had to do was indulge in something I wanted to do anyway.

Because some of you know me well. Very well. Don't fidget, Stanley, I enjoyed our mornings together. I don't blame you for giving me the best assignments. That's what friends do for each other. And I wasn't lying when I told you that you knew how to please me like no other man.

I still remember—especially now, when memory suffices for

touch—what it was like to walk out of my office, nonchalant and seemingly bored or distracted by demands. I would be nude beneath my proper gray skirt, keeping that particular secret like a card tucked away for a winning hand. (Not enough women wear stockings these days, and men seem to respond so well to that ridiculous bit of hosiery.) I'd duck into the conference room on the fifth floor and close the door against curious secretaries and clerks. And wait for you there, my heart beating a little faster as the heady world of business hummed around us. Then I'd hear you come in at last.

I remember feeling brash as I lifted up my skirt for the shock of showing off, becoming aroused before we'd even begun. Your eyes, quick kisses, then your hot mouth and clever tongue delving deep: I reveled in it. Your hands clutching my thighs, pulling me closer, famished for a woman. Stanley, believe me, I wasn't joking about the squirming, or the coming, either. It was so hard to keep quiet, but that added to the enjoyment, didn't it?

And then of course, I didn't mind turning around for you. I was always wet and more than happy to let you fuck me after I'd come, squirming against your insistent tongue. And you were always primed for me after a session with your head between my legs. I'd lean against the conference table, spreading my thighs, feeling like some model in a magazine, playing the roles you men expect. Part of me liked that a lot, doing what those bimbos only act out. I played the slut well when I had to—something in me was excited as hell by it. It was about sex, but it was also about power...using it, buying it—-and surrendering it. Who had the power? You or me?

I could speculate about that forever these days, lying back on my bed, hands cupping a breast, pouting for a suck, fingers wiggling into my slippery folds. Thinking about the illicit plea-sures back then. You'd be almost panting behind me, unzipping yourself, hand on your cock, transformed into something primal. Pushing that warm erection into me, greed and haste burnishing everything. Urgency made it more exciting.

I could almost have loved you, Stanley. Almost.

I have needs, gentlemen, just like you. Appetites. But I never was a cartoon temptress. I was always discreet—except where bravado would be more effective—and I never was a threat to your wives. I didn't want what they had; I wanted something completely different from you. And I played fair, didn't I? I gave back as good as I got, both in what I gave and in the job I did.

Some of you don't like me, and that's all right. I didn't like all of you. Some of you didn't take what I offered. I respect that, and would never hold a polite "No, thank you" against you. And for some of you, I was just the wrong flavor. Who? Oh, no. That's their business, not yours.

So that's how I got here. I fucked my way up, enjoying a smorgasbord of men along the way. Greg in accounting always did my reports first, and he gave me such good advice about where to cut the fat and where to prime the machine that soon my division became stellar. That got noticed. I thanked him, of course. He loves blow jobs, and I don't mind them, either.

He'd groan, "No," but never actually try to stop me, gripping the armrests of his chair and grimacing as I teased him, crouching down, talking dirty until he was stiff. He was as appalled by us as he was delighted. I loved opening his belt and getting it out, his flesh stiff with arousal, the man beneath the suit emerging, taking over. The carpeting in the office I wasn't so crazy about, but I could get comfortable down there, closing my eyes beneath the fluorescents and imagining we were someplace else. I'd lick at his cock, rigid as the laws of numbers, sliding him in and out. If I said I didn't enjoy it, I'd be lying.

I'd take Greg over the edge, then leave him there, limp and

satiated. I'd spend the rest of my day wanting more, the taste of his semen in my mouth. A secret.

Work and sex. Lucky for me, my career gave me both.

Of course, if I'd been nothing more than a good lay, I'd have gotten nowhere. But I had ambition and brains, too, along with the body and appetite for pleasure. It's a lucky combination, and it's served me well. I may have slept my way up the corporate ladder and into my titles, but I know damned well that ability kept me there. Sex just helped slide things along more smoothly. Getting to know my colleagues—and superiors—a little better. To make sure they would remember me.

Eventually, I reached VP of production, reporting directly to the company president and no one else. The day Griffith Morgeson announced my assumption of the title, I sat in the boardroom, eyes directed modestly down to the walnut table, losing myself in the reflections on the surface. Idle thoughts occupied me while middle-aged voices droned on. As on other days when I got an edge by being a little whorish, I wore no panties under my silk suit, and desire, my silent partner, distracted me.

I waited, crossing and uncrossing my legs, until I thought I'd just have to slip my hand down there and rub all around until I came. I wanted to thank him—Griff—for the promotion in a very special way. How would I do it? Naked, in his office? My bare skin would be sweetly pink against his elegant upholstery. How could he say no? Surrounded by the unceasing momentum of commerce and propriety, the immediacy of lust would be even richer. I knew that well enough.

Or right there on the boardroom table? I squeezed my thighs together, cradling my want like a cupped flame in a storm. The table. I wanted to spread myself out, stripped of all my clothes, and share my success with everyone. Wouldn't that have been a fun way to make a Thursday meeting memorable? I couldn't, of course, but I fantasized about it for weeks afterward. The idea kept me wet for days: imagining a dozen scenarios with me brazen and naked on that hefty slab of corporate wood. Each of you, taking a turn. Can you imagine that? I could. I liked the sex. And I liked the attention.

I know what it's like to feel your eyes on me, like a hundred softly whispered compliments, even as you listen to me talk about mergers and strategy, staffing and consolidation. I relish the covert glance up from the report I've distributed, hungry on my breasts, hips, and ass. I don't blame you. You wonder if my nipples are neat, or big and bold, if I shave away the curls between my legs. Are my tits as nice out of my bra as they look in this sweater? I arch my back a little. I'm not above using what I've got to keep your attention. And yes—they are.

I imagine your daydreams. You've told me the nature of such things, decoded masculine speculation in postcoital confession. What would my ass feel like cupped in your hands as you slide my skirt up, your cock hard, excited ever more by the forbidden? Transgression is exciting. You watch me talk, and wonder what my mouth would look like circling you, engorged, on the cusp of release. It would look exciting, but it would feel even better. I know how to use my tongue.

You've heard whispers of rumors, shadows of words, all about me, and it intrigues you. You wonder if they're true. Domesticity is dull. So is this meeting. You imagine sliding your cock right into the velvet grip of me. Clench like a fist.

I behave impeccably, act the professional, tilting toward prim. Desire is pointless. There is no chance.

Then I give you a smile and you feel like it's your birthday.

Eventually, I fucked my way to the president. Ascending. Because power is sexy: wielding it and being in its presence. I liked it, liked that scent of power like a whiff of high voltage, a heady thrum of something you can't quite see but can't help feel.

Griff was a widower and a fairly nice guy. He was vigorous for his years, healthy and active, and I liked him. Company president, chief of staff. He had charm, rugged good looks, an outdoorsman's vitality, despite being a corporate executive, trapped in a world of desks and long lunches. He worked out regularly, and more women than I considered him attractive. Power suited him. A nice guy? By then, maybe, competition and determination had worked their way out of his system (along with most, but not all, of his wild oats). He'd been mellowed by age, success, time, and the first grandchild.

I was still hungry, though.

Hungry enough that when we took a meeting, I held his eyes too long. I smiled. I let my skirt rise like his hopes, and I left my blouse open to possibility. He wasn't stupid, and he could have any woman he chose. I was attracted to him and let him know it. *Choose me*, I willed. I'd make it so. I packaged my charms discreetly and presented them quietly. The obvious tricks I'd used on some of you wouldn't work on him. But I knew with me, it would be different, and maybe he did, too. Almost a meeting of equals.

And he still had appetite for what I could offer: pleasure, along with a frisson of the forbidden. You know that combination. Guilt's a wonderful spice, just a pinch will do. Naughtiness is so very piquant.

One miserable afternoon in November, I decided the time was right to make my move. I asked to see Griff, alone, timing it for a quiet afternoon in a dull time of the year. I entered and sat in front of his desk, and he waited, tapping his pen. For the first time, I was nervous. This was the company president, after all. I'd never dared climb so high.

But I had prepared for that morning, and it started the old sway of desire, like plucking a string and hearing it resonate long after.

It was dim in his office, the rain muting the day. Griff's desk lamp was on, casting a warm, intimate glow. I wanted to be in that golden circle of light. He'd shucked his jacket and rolled his shirtsleeves up. His arms were strong and muscular, still tanned. He'd been climbing mountains that autumn. He still wore his wedding ring, and I liked that touch of sentiment. Iron-gray hair brushed his forehead. He watched me look at him as the silence built between us. His strength—and his patience—were like granite. Solid. Gray. Griffith. His tie was dark red, a burgundy like spilled wine. Wine. I should have asked him out for a drink, instead, done this over a glass or three in some dark and inviting place. But it was too late.

The silence lengthened, and he, never a fool, waited, letting me be the first to speak. My heart was beating louder, I'd swear, and new nerves fluttered in my belly. One brow began to rise as the seconds built, and I wondered: under his white shirt, was his chest hairy? Of course it would be. I thought of brushing my breasts, nipples puckered and awakened, against that springy hair and the warmth of his skin. And just like that, I relaxed. I wanted him.

He finally spoke, filling the silence. "What can I do for you, Marianne?"

"You," I said, and stood.

Instinct took over. I hadn't really planned how I'd offer myself.

Then I knew: Nude. Now.

I pretended that I knew what I was doing and began to unbutton my blouse. Griff's hand went still, the pen resting in midtap. One button to three to them all, showing the lace I'd chosen. The blouse fell and his mouth opened.

I unzipped my skirt, let it drop, and got the bra off with minimum fumbling. My nipples hardened at my audacity. I'd either be fired or committed to the hospital downtown. But success—and prior experience—carried me through. Panties briefer than a winter day slid down my thighs. His eyes clouded, and I liked it.

I stripped in his office, slowly and completely, until I stood before his big desk, naked, completely nude. How did they describe the effects of an assault? Shock and awe? Yes, that's the effect it had on Griff, but in a nice way.

It excited me, too. By the time my panties slipped from one ankle, I was wet.

And he was hard.

I stood there, gift and reward, offering myself. He gave an inarticulate cry and was around that desk faster than a nervous blink. For a minute, I thought he was going to run right past me and out of his office, barking for security. Doom. Then the lock clicked, and I knew he wanted it as much as I wanted to give it.

In seconds, Griff had me down on the floor, my knees up, and he straddled me, shaking his head. Bemusement, amusement, disbelief. And lust. I could see the hard-on in his gray trousers, and it pleased me enormously. I couldn't wait to touch it. His skin would be hot against my tongue. The throb of him, caught up like a leaf in a swollen spring river, in wanting.

Stripped of my corporate pretense, I was his. My skin warm against the carpet in his office. My nudity turned me to honey inside. Pinned beneath him, exactly where I wanted to be.

He knelt over me, conqueror, denying me the role of seductress, taking charge. Good. Then when he looked back, whatever happened would burn as a mutual event. I had provoked, but he seized the bait. Griff didn't speak, he just looked down at me, gray wool trousers trying to hold back the evidence of his arousal. I'd never felt more naked, more exposed in my life, but it was all right, I knew it. My nipples were hard—exhilaration, fear, or desire, or it may have been a combination of all those turbulent feelings flying through me. He touched my right nipple, as if considering what was offered to him, rolling it slowly with his thumb and finger. I moaned.

"Okay," he muttered. "Okay."

He unzipped his trousers, got his belt open, and his nakedness broke out to join mine. His cock thrust out, weighty and potent, just like the man. I eyed it, longing. I was all promise, entirely consent, and knew no foreplay was required. My undressing had been enough. For both of us.

In but a moment, he was between my legs, and he swallowed the nipple he'd touched, sucking hard, pushing his erection into me. His tie dangled down for a moment, then red silk was crushed in our coupling. My bare thighs slid along the fine weave of his trousers, and his cock made me whole. Held down on the office carpet with his body, with nothing to soften his thrusts, Griff took me. Fast, furious, and hard, and he found me molten within.

I'd been ready all morning, ready for weeks, and slid up to meet each thrust, wetting him. He quickened, I hung on, climax as inevitable as sunrise. He sucked my nipple, frantic, then reared up, pounding into me, his face stripped of convention's mask, naked in his pleasure. His thrusts created my release. Like a figure on horseback emerging from a sandstorm, chaos coalesced everything to a single thing: I was just about to... "Griff," I prayed, hoarse, the compulsion to tell. He fucked me. "I'm coming...."

His kiss silenced me, and I soared, biting his tongue, hot and wet.

He followed but a moment later, stifling his own cry into my hair. I tried, as always, to feel the moment the rush of semen began but couldn't quite tell when the first erupted or the last ended. Only by his slowing thrusts, his ragged breath, his last shudder, did I know when his release had swept through him.

"What do you want?" he asked when we were done. I floated back to shore, aware of the carpet against my skin, the ceiling of Griff's office, the sound of business continuing beyond his door, our interlude. The phone had rung on his desk unanswered; soft knocks at the door were ignored. I pictured his secretary outside, fuming, and hoped she was discreet.

"Nothing," I replied, and maybe, just at that moment, that was even true.

We had an affair. It was almost the best time of my life. I had it all. I was fucking the boss and loving every minute of it. I never asked for more than he chose to give. I never pestered him to make a commitment, to spend the holidays with me, to buy me things. I didn't need him for that, and I liked my private time, too. I was still an executive with plenty of my own responsibilities and constant demands on my time. I liked his companionship, and he was a fine partner in bed. If being on such good terms with the company president helped me in my career, then so be it. He got a lot of enjoyment out of our time together. I played fair.

I never asked for more than what he offered. Eventually, he offered a lot.

I'd fucked my way to the top floor, the penthouse suite of a glass-steel-and-more-glass building filled with egos as big as monuments, and I went right through that ceiling. On my knees, sure, or on my back, or at my desk, I didn't care which helped get me there.

He offered everything. Gold ring: That was my prize. I was indecisive for days. Then not. We were married.

And it was good. I knew there would be no children, and I knew he was used to living life on his terms. I knew I was stepping into a role another woman had originated, but I was nothing like his first wife, and even his children allowed him the consolation of a second marriage.

Then, as you know, Griff died. Heart attack, at the summer place. And yes, the rumors about that are true, too. He went out with a smile on his face, because he'd just finished fucking me. It had been a bit more enthusiastic than usual, and he'd rolled over at the end, complaining about being exhausted. Smug, I thought I'd worn him out. He stepped away for a cigar on the deck at sunset. And that's where he went.

Funny, he didn't call for me, or try to save himself. He died well, I think. He didn't linger; he didn't become pathetic.

And he was where he wanted to be, although at his desk would have been just as likely, considering Griff had a hard time letting go of anything that he'd worked hard to get.

So he was gone. I found that I missed him far more than I'd expected to. I missed that son of a bitch a lot. I thought it had all been about opportunity and bargains, about doing what I had to do. Then why did it hurt so much to be without him? My body craved what he'd been giving me regularly—that vigor was expressed in more places than the boardroom and the golf course—I missed that, too.

I still wanted to fuck, but now I also wanted to wake up in the morning and find the same person on the other pillow day after day. Griff. That I wanted a person on the other pillow surprised me. I haven't been that sentimental in years, but I got used to having someone...around.

And the thing of it is? Almost any one of you guys would be happy to step up and fill the president's shoes—and his bed. But I don't want you anymore. And there's nowhere to go now.

Anyway. I know it's an unusual resignation, but there you go, boys. Cream in your Armanis, jump in your handmade shoes. Someone younger and hungrier can take my place now. I did get what I'd wanted, and I left my mark. Money? You always ask about money. Well, I've got enough of that for the rest of my days. I don't care.

Work? My heart's not in it anymore. It's time to retire.

It's lonely at the top.

ON THE 37TH FLOOR

Tulsa Brown

B ut, Lise, you promised you'd go to the Christmas party with
me."

"Darrel, that was before we broke up," I said.

"I told everyone a month ago you'd be coming."

"You should have found another date."

"I haven't been well." Darrel sniffled. "Besides, you know I
miss you." His voice tugged at me, a dog pawing my leg under
the table.

I sighed. "I'll see if I can find a dress."

Darrel Groening was lank-haired and lean, forever on the
verge of a cold. I'd met him the previous spring, and within
fifteen minutes, I'd known he wasn't the right species, never
mind the right person. Yet I'd limped through a whole excruci-
ating summer with him and taken two more months to break it
off. That was because I'd been born in Trent, Minnesota, where
women had five more commandments than everyone else:

1. Never accept a compliment.

2. Never refuse a gracious invitation.

3. Never pay full price.

4. Never complain.

5. Never break your word.

They weren't written down anywhere, but growing up I'd heard them more often than the other ten. When I'd moved to New York at the age of twenty-five, I didn't have to pack them—they were already under my skin.

Darrel was pretty sharp. He not only figured out the extra commandments, he learned to play them like a video game. Extending number one into number five was a particular skill of his. And sex? Well, he was lucky there was number four.

The party came too soon. I found myself in the corporate ballroom of a Manhattan office building one night in mid-December, against my will and entirely with my consent. Darrel put on a brave front for a man with terminal sinus congestion, and he wheeled me around the room on his arm, showing me off like a new watch. I was alarmed to discover how much people already knew about me but even more irritated by his introduction.

"This is my girlfriend, Lise. It rhymes with 'please.'"

I smiled through gritted teeth.

"My, she is a little thing," big, beautiful people boomed at me. The term in Trent, Minnesota, is *slight,* as in "slight women shouldn't wear loud colors," and "slight women should never look too happy—it makes all the other women miserable."

There was no danger of that. Wearing a simple satin dress in pastel blue with dyed-to-match sandals, I was lost in the swirl of glamorous strangers, a direct consequence of commandment number three. Surrounded by chic cocktail black, I felt like an escaped bridesmaid. I downed two glasses of wine and wondered how I could feign illness without igniting Darrel's competitive streak.

"Ooh, boy, watch out for this one," he whispered abruptly in my ear. "Major corporate bitch at three o'clock."

Even from halfway across the room, Maybird Howe was the most extraordinary-looking woman I'd ever seen. A tall, generously proportioned woman, she broke enough rules of propriety to make the women of Trent howl. Full breasts swelled dangerously over her low-cut gown, and her bare arms were nearly as large as my thighs—and certainly more curvaceous. She walked toward us in a slow, swaying undulation, her gold and red beaded dress shimmering. She looked like Mardi Gras at night, a rave of color against her dark, abundant flesh.

I was mesmerized at first, too intimidated to speak. Maybird seemed to float on a smooth cloud of confidence, and even her small talk sparkled with wit. When she looked at me, I felt I was standing in a sunbeam. Where did a woman come from, I wondered, to have this kind of radiance?

Darrel ducked away shortly after the introductions, supposedly to get me another drink. Maybird showed no sign of leaving, although I was sure I was boring her to blindness. I struggled to find the voice I knew I used to have.

"Is Maybird really your name?" I asked finally.

She arched an eyebrow and tilted her head. "Is that limp noodle really your fiancé?"

"No! Oh, God, no." Is that what he'd been telling people? I fluttered and flapped like an alarmed bird, desperate that she know the truth. A slow smile lit up her round, calm face.

"I'm glad. His office is only on the fifteenth floor, you know. A splendid creature like you should be dating well above the twentieth."

The words made me hum with warm, unexpected pleasure, but she'd nailed me directly on number one. I backed away from the compliment so fast I could have knocked someone over.

Maybird watched me, still smiling, yet there was a new intensity to her liquid, lioness eyes.

"Come up to my office. I want my view to enjoy you," she said.

Her view to enjoy me? Was I drunk, or was she teasing me? Yet I did want to go with her, more than I'd wanted anything in a long time.

"Well, maybe for a few minutes," I said.

Riding the elevator up to the thirty-seventh floor, I was engulfed by Maybird's presence, the dizzying scent of her perfume—chrysanthemums or another lush, heavy flower. I found myself gazing at her gown, wondering what her generous hip would feel like if I ran my hand over it, the soft press of flesh under the sleek, nubby surface of the beadwork. I was shocked that I wasn't shocked.

She had magnetic key cards for everything—the elevator, the closed hallway, her own office. Leading me through this last door, she switched on two wall sconces, but the rich oak paneling and leather furniture were already softly illuminated. All of Manhattan was lighting up this room.

"Oh," I breathed. The window was the length of one wall, a magnificent, glittering panorama. It drew me over without a thought, and I stood, hands on the waist-high sill, steadying myself against the thrilling rush of vertigo.

"Now do you see why you should date above the twentieth floor?" Maybird asked. "Beauty deserves beauty."

I turned with a self-conscious laugh, prepared to argue, but the nervous noise died in my throat. She was very close now, and I was silenced by the sienna landscape in front of me, the near-nakedness of her bare arms and plunging cleavage. Maybird leaned her generous ass against the edge of the desk, beadwork rubbing the wood in an exciting crystalline growl.

She smiled. "Take your shoes off, little miss, if they hurt your feet."

The name nipped me, a tiny bite in a secret place. Yet she was right—I was sliding forward in my cheap sandals, toes cramping. I stepped out of them with relief, dropping three inches in front of her.

"And your stockings."

"Pardon?"

"When you stand on my desk, I don't want you to slip."

Had I heard right? I was bewildered. I glanced out the plate-glass window again, at the vast spread of buildings glowing in the December night. I could see right into the lighted offices across the street, the abandoned desks and file cabinets clearly defined in the hard fluorescence. And if I could see them...

Maybird moved in closer and stroked my hair, easing it off my neck. She left her warm hand on my bare shoulder, and the heat permeated my whole body.

"They've all gone home. And if someone did see, do you think they'd recognize you tomorrow on the sidewalk? You're safe, you're free." Her smile was superior, glimmering with seasons of experience. "I want my view to enjoy you, little miss."

That name again. My sex lips were thickening between my thighs. I felt a long way from Trent, emboldened by two glasses of wine and the touch of this strong, exciting woman. How old was she? Thirty-five? Forty? All I knew was that her voice held me in thrall. I wanted to fall into it, like a river, and be carried away. I turned discreetly and reached under my skirt to slide the pantyhose off. For a brazen second I thought of slipping out of my panties, too, but...no.

My bare legs whispered in surprise against each other. Maybird held out her hand for the soft wad of my stockings, which she tossed into the wastepaper basket. I stared after them, stung by a parting shot of conscience. They'd cost fifteen dollars.

"Up you go."

I stepped onto the leather chair, then up to the gleaming wooden desk top, straightening slowly, lightheaded with the sudden height and strange perspective. It didn't seem like the same room anymore. I was facing the office's back wall as Maybird's voice drifted out to me.

"Turn around to the window. Tell me what you see."

I swiveled with tiny, cautious steps, bare feet sticking to the polished surface. Then I laughed, exhilarated.

"Oh, my God, it's beautiful! It's like the Milky Way." From this new angle, the hard edge of the sill vanished from my field of vision. All I could see were endless lights, a galaxy glittering on and on. If I stared forward, there was no office and no window, and my perception of depth dissolved. I was simply floating in the lights, as one of them. It was magical and strangely...familiar. For an instant I was a child again, lying under the vast prairie night sky, believing I was one of the stars.

"Yes, the Milky Way," Maybird murmured. Then: "Take your dress off. Let it fall to your feet."

My clit swelled at the unthinkable wickedness. To bare my body in front of a full-length window, simply for another's woman's pleasure, so that she could...what?

Enjoy the view.

"*Now*, little miss."

The demand in her voice was thrilling. My heart fluttered as I reached behind and grasped the tab, the zipper teeth parting in a purr of acquiescence. My pussy was slick, the engorged lips pressing against the taut crotch of my cotton panties. I wondered what color I'd chosen this morning, and if it would suit her.

A rustle told me Maybird was still waiting. I shrugged off

the tiny straps and let the fabric fall into a tumble of blue satin around my ankles.

"Ahh." Her sigh was a croon of appreciation, a caress along my naked back. The sound spoke to my nipples, which finished hardening in the open air, aching to be touched. A tiny corner of my mind was aghast, unable to believe I was truly standing here, exposed to the night city. Yet the rest of me wasn't thinking at all. I was simply part of the sky, a wet and throbbing star, beautiful, powerful, ravenous.

The swish of her gown pulled me back to earth. I didn't dare look down as her breath swept over the back of my legs, but when she opened her mouth in a luscious kiss on my calf, a hot V of pleasure shot up through my womb. I swayed.

"I might fall," I whispered.

"All right, sit down."

I lowered myself to the desktop, letting her pull my dress away so it wouldn't be crushed. She shook out the wrinkles and crossed the room to drape it carefully over a chair. I sat on the desk with my legs dangling, a child who'd been perched on the counter to stay out of the way. I desperately wanted to touch myself but didn't dare.

Maybird sauntered back to me, her holiday gown swinging with its own luxurious weight, her brown eyes gleaming in a tease. A laughing lioness. As she drew up against the desk, I spread my knees wide to encompass her ample hips and reached up to embrace her. She caught my wrists and firmly returned my hands to my sides, palms flat on the desk.

"I have a ruler in my drawer," she said pleasantly. "Don't make me get it out."

My clit throbbed at the startling thought.

Maybird kissed me, a sweet sucking of astonishing power. I felt as if she were drawing my sex up into her mouth. She cupped my breasts, rolling my hard nipples into tight points. I spread my legs painfully as I tried to inch closer to her curving belly, a vain hope of rubbing my pussy against her beaded dress. I moaned with mindless want, a hungry little animal.

At last, she stroked me between the legs with her thumb, a stripe of pleasure that made me gasp.

"My, those panties are nice and wet, little miss."

"Oh, yes…oh, please." I tried not to whimper.

"Lie down on my desk."

I stretched out on the spacious wooden surface, and it was as hard and uncomfortable as I feared—for half a minute. After that, I forgot about it completely. Maybird unzipped her own gown and eased her huge, soft breasts from their confinement, bending over to gather me into an earthy embrace. I suckled on one and stroked the other, nursing eagerly on the plump, heavy flesh. She stripped my panties off and pushed my knees to my chest, my pussy a wet crescent that she opened, stroked, and teased.

Finally, she plunged two fingers deep into my cunt, her thumb still lodged against my erect clit. For a fleeting second, I thought of how it must look through her window, the pale shock of my slender schoolgirl's body curled up in her dark arms, nursing on her like a child, getting fucked by her strong hand. But I was beyond caring. I wasn't of this earth—my planet was pleasure, rocking, sucking, moaning.

Coming. My inner muscles clutched, spasms of bliss shaking me in pulsing white waves. I ground and twisted against her hand, thrusting my orgasm over one crest, then another, riding it greedily, joy bursting in my tits and toes. And all the while I was enveloped by the softest pillow in the world.

It was so strange to get dressed again. The concept of clothes and a life outside this room seemed alien to me. I glanced in the wastebasket at my stockings, and it was hard to remember what they were for, never mind that I'd sighed over their loss.

I noticed Maybird watching me, her eyes occasionally glancing at the desktop, the place where I'd shed myself and become one of the stars. I was haunted by the mystery. What had she seen in me or heard in my voice? How had she known what the view would do to me? What she would do to me?

"Where are you from?" I asked.

Maybird's face was as calm and luminous as polished oak, but there was a glimmer in her eyes. "Oh, nowhere, really. Just a small city in the Midwest."

I felt a clutch. "Not…Trent."

The game was up, and she smiled broadly. "No, I'm from Arthur, Minnesota. But it's very close, hardly a day's run—"

"—for a lame dog," I finished the colloquialism for her, stunned. The revelation opened up inside me. No wonder Maybird had my number. She had them all, one through five—the damning extra commandments we'd both grown up with. And yet here she was in front of me, sensual, self-assured, beaming beauty and quiet power. Radiance. It gave me a shot of hope that bubbled out in a laugh.

"You know, I don't think I'm going to say goodbye to my 'fiancé' on the way out," I said.

"No, I don't think you are." Maybird extended her hand and I took it, and we stepped into the polished hallway, two celestial bodies glowing in a new night.

HAVE A NICE DAY

Mike Kimera

Here is the message I sent you on the beeper: "Open the box in private—but open it at once."

Five minutes later, at eleven-thirty, UPS delivers a parcel marked PERSONAL to your desk at work. Everyone notices as you go to the bathroom immediately to open it.

It contains a note, a condom, and a large black dildo—one of those anatomically correct but way-out-of-scale dildos, all veins and ridges, made out of silicone so that they bend and feel warm to the touch. It looks huge in your hand. You find yourself playing with it, feeling the weight in the palm of your hand. Without thinking, you rub the head against your cheek. Then you remember the note. It says: "Take off your panties. Fold them and put them in your purse. Slide the condom over the dildo, and push the dildo all the way into your cunt. Do *not* fuck yourself with it. Go to our table at Starbucks at 12:15."

Your cunt is very wet. *Surely,* you think, *this huge dildo will never fit.* Then you realize you will have to go back to the office with it inside you and wait until it's time to walk to the coffee shop around the corner. You think of how this monster will feel in your cunt as you walk. You notice that you are squeezing the rubber cock in your hand. With sudden determination, you take off your panties—red silk today—fold them, and put them in your purse.

You have just ripped the foil on the condom when you hear people enter the toilet. You don't have time to wait. You roll the condom down over the black cock in your hands—shit, this feels so real you half expect it to spit come at you—hoping no one will recognize that condom smell. You put one foot up on the toilet bowl, open yourself as wide as you can, and start to push the monster in.

Someone enters the stall next to yours. You are struggling to take it all inside you. Trying not to be heard. Trying not to just fuck yourself crazy with this invader. You get most of it inside you. Two inches protrude. You sit on the toilet seat and, balancing on the tip of the dildo, you push hard. It slides in slowly, making you groan.

The black dildo is now deep in your cunt. You pull down your skirt and step out of the cubicle. In the mirror, you see that your nipples are very prominent and that your legs are slightly parted, causing your skirt to rise up a little. People are bound to notice something in the office

You return to your desk. The beeper goes. You read, "How does it feel?"

The beeper goes again. "Cross your legs."

You obey and feel the rubber cock move inside you. Three minutes till you leave for Starbucks. A colleague comes to your desk and asks you if you'd like to go to lunch. You think he's looking at your hard nipples. Can he smell you? You want to look at his cock to see if it's hard, but you dare not risk it. You smile and decline his offer.

Walking has never been so difficult. Although you know how tightly held the cock is, you worry it will slip out. You feel as though your legs are spread wide as you walk. Your hips sway slightly more than normal. This attracts attention. You try to hurry and suddenly have to stand still. The pressure is too much. You walk slowly to Starbucks. The beeper goes: "Don't turn around. I'm watching you. Fits snugly, doesn't it?" You reach Starbucks as you finish reading the message.

Our table is taken. A beautiful black woman in a stylish bright yellow business suit is sitting there. You turn to look for me when the woman smiles, stands, and embraces you.

"Jenny," she cries, hugging you to her. She is six feet, slim, with long black hair, a wide mouth, bright teeth, high cheekbones. There is no blouse under the business jacket.

As she hugs you, she whispers: "It's a very *big* dildo isn't it Jenny? Sit very close to me, raise your skirt so your bare ass is on the chair, and keep your legs a little apart. Your man sent me." She kisses you on both cheeks and sits down. You are shocked. I've never done this to you before.

Your beeper goes, "DO AS SHE SAYS." When you look up, you see that her eyes are focused on your nipples. Seeing your look, she smiles and licks her lips. You sit. The shiny aluminum chair is cold against your flesh. She moves her chair closer to yours and, as she passes you a latte with her left hand, her right hand slides up your thigh to your cunt.

"Don't spill the coffee on this nice skirt," she says and looks you in the eye as her fingers trace your swollen cunt lips and feel the butt of the dildo at the entrance to your pussy. You sit absolutely still.

She pushes gently on the dildo, but it doesn't move. Her

fingers stroke back down your thigh in slow circles. She brings her fingers to her lips and licks them. "I love a tight, wet cunt," she says. "I was told you would be good." You look down at your coffee. "Nice nipples, too. Glad to see there's no bra…. I'm going to use you, Jenny—with your permission—I *do* have your permission, don't I?" She pauses.

You look up. "Yes, you have my permission to use me…. I would like that."

She makes a call on her cell phone, and a white stretch limo pulls up. She leads you by the hand to the limo. You worry about getting in without flashing your dildo-filled cunt at the world. People know you here. She solves the problem for you. Once the door is open, she pushes you hard on the back of the head, and you fall into the limo face first, ass in the air. As you scramble for balance you hear the sound of yourself coming. The video in the limo shows you being fucked by me and coming hard.

"Don't just lie there, Jenny. Take a seat and watch the show—I've seen it twice. My name's Lily, by the way." You look up and then past her and finally you see me sitting in the center of a bench seat. I look at you but say nothing.

Lily lifts you easily and places you in the center of the bench seat opposite. She ties each of your ankles to a car door, spreading your legs so wide the muscles on the inside of your thighs tremble. Lily pushes back your skirt so that your whole ass is visible. She lifts both of your hands above your head and ties them to a headrest. Your back is arched. Only your ass is on the seat. You sway slightly as the car moves.

Lily sits beside me, and we both watch you. The video is on loop and starts with you on the floor, tied, with my cock in your mouth. Lily kisses me and unzips my cock. I push her head down on it while keeping my eyes on you. The black dildo is visible in your swollen cunt. Already, I can smell your juices. Your eyes plead with me for attention.

I pull Lily's head off my cock and push her toward you. "You're getting the seat damp, Jenny," Lily says. Her fingers trace the outline of your wet cunt lips around the dildo butt. You moan and look away. She kneels between your legs and licks your clit. Your ass bounces on the seat.

"Show her," I say.

Lily takes off the yellow jacket. Her breasts are very round. They both have large gold nipple rings. She hefts one breast in her hand and licks the nipple with her long tongue. Shimmying out of the skirt, she exposes a shaved pussy and a tight, muscled ass. She is wearing a harness around her hips and between her legs. Seeing you look at it, she points to a ring on the harness just above her clit. "This is what the butt of that dildo slots into, Jenny. I'm going to have such fun fucking you with it. Maybe we should see how well it fits your ass."

You look at Lily, licking your lips. "Come fuck me with your big cock, bitch," you moan, your hips swaying and your pussy gripping the dildo.

I grin at your response. "I told you she was good, Lily. Enjoy her."

Lily licks her way up your thighs. Her tongue penetrates your ass. She pushes deeply into you. Her strong tongue passes through your rose. She sucks hard. Her large lips move up. She takes the dildo in her teeth and pulls it back an inch. She slots it into the belt.

"Fuck me," you say and push yourself forward, pressing the dildo against her mound. You feel the huge dildo slide deep into you as Lily rams it in and out of you. Bouncing your hips off the car seat to meet each thrust, you push back on the dildo so she feels it against her clit. Both of you moan as she fucks you. Your bodies are covered with sweat as she pushes faster and deeper into your hot cunt.

I reach over and pull on her nipple rings as I tweak your tit. I push two fingers up your ass as Lily pushes hard, burying the dildo deep in your cunt. You pull on the ropes as you feel the dildo stretch your tight pussy, then push back on it, making Lily moan. Faster and faster she fucks into you, your body squirming as I ram my fingers up your hot ass. Lily pushes deep into you, grinding her hips against you as she comes. I shove my fingers farther into your ass and pinch your clit, making you scream as you come.

I release your hands and legs, sit on the seat you have made damp, and then retie your hands behind your back, leaving your legs free as you kneel in front of me. Grabbing your head, I force my cock into your wet mouth. You feel Lily's hands stroking your back as your lips slide up and down my hard cock. I push your head down onto my cock. It lodges with comfortable familiarity deep in your throat.

A shiver runs through your body as you groan against my cock and Lily pushes her fingers into your ass. Looking into my eyes, you suck me hard and deep, with your tongue twirling around my cock. Lily fingers your ass as I fuck my cock in and out of your mouth. I hear you moan and feel you jerk as Lily pushes the big dildo up your tight ass. I watch as the big black dildo disappears, spreading your asshole as inch by inch it sinks into your tight tunnel. Your ass squirms prettily as Lily impales you on the huge rod. Reflexively, your ass ring tightens, fighting to keep out the dildo that's splitting you.

I keep your mouth on my cock as you arch your back, trying to lift your head up and scream. Lily grins at me as she twists the dildo in your ass, making your body jerk. I watch as she pulls it out until just the crown is surrounded by your ass ring. I nod my head at her, and with one forceful stroke she buries the dildo deep in your ass as I push down on your head and flex my hips, forcing my cock fully into your throat. You feel my cock pulse as I come down your throat. "Drink it," I say and feel your throat tighten as you swallow my semen.

I untie your hands and hug you to me. Lily has detached the dildo from her harness, leaving it buried in your ass.

"Help me tie Lily," I say. Lily lies back in the seat, taking up more of it than you did. We spread her legs so wide the pink inside her slit is visible. With clever knots you tie her outstretched legs, making her lean forward slightly. You kneel back to look at her.

I raise your hands above your head and slip off your top. It is the first time Lily has seen your breasts. From behind you I cup them, kissing your neck, working on the hard nipples, while you smile at Lily. The elegant gold nipple clamps close brutally over each of your nipples in turn. You bite your lip as I connect each of your clamps to one of Lily's nipple rings by five inches of gold chain. You are very close to one another now but not touching.

I pull you backward on your heels and then farther, until your breasts and hers are both stretched and the little gold chains are taut. Lily's eyes go wide and I realize she is a screamer. I reach into your purse and find the panties you placed there earlier. "Use these to gag her," I say and let go of you.

You climb between Lily's legs and place the gusset of your panties against her tongue, filling her mouth with them. Then you kiss her throat, hands resting on her breasts.

"Lily likes to be fisted," I say, "but she's never been fisted in her little brown hole. I think you could put one of your small hands in each hole at the same time, don't you, Jenny?" Lily starts to struggle, shaking her head and jiggling the chains that bind you together.

You make eye contact with her, smile wickedly, and say, "I would enjoy that." You kiss Lily on the lips and whisper in her ear: "I do have your permission to use you, don't I, Lily? To use you harder than you've ever been used before?" Lily pauses, feeling your tongue trace its way down her neck. She nods briefly but will not look at you.

I smear K-Y over your hands and wrists. You slowly work your fingers into her rear hole, one at a time, until you can get your entire hand inside of her. Lily thrashes like a dying fish as you slide into her past your wrist. You pull back a little, then you thrust your hand all the way in. You place your left hand on her cunt. The lips are swollen. Pink is clearly visible. Juices are running from her cunt to where your arm is buried in her ass. You laugh and slide your hand easily into her pussy.

I watch your delight as you discover that you can rub your hands together. Even muffled by the gag, Lily's screams are loud. I turn on the stereo. "Wanna lover with a slow hand" drowns out Lily's moans. My cock is hard again. I slip it into your cunt from behind, feeling how the dildo in your ass squeezes me. You fuck Lily to the rhythm of my cock in your cunt. Lily's body is now covered in sweat.

I know I won't last long inside you. Your whole cunt is massaging my cock. On the outward pull of your arms you lean back so you can pull Lily's breasts with your own. On the inward stroke you push deep into her and lean your breasts against her. With each stroke your cunt massages my cock. You are close to orgasm now. My hand finds your bud and coaxes it. As you come, you push deeper yet into Lily and lie gasping against her breasts.

I pull out of you and wank over Lily's face. She hardly notices; she is coming in both holes at once, trapping your hands in her flesh.

Still with your hands in her, you lick my come from her face and neck. For a few moments, you are lost to the sensations of licking and tasting. I know that you are completely focused now.

"Time to go back to work, Jenny." You look at me, confused. I kiss your forehead and pull your hands from Lily. I hand you Wet Ones to clean yourself with.

You reach to remove the dildo from your ass. "Leave it there. I'll beep you to say when you can remove it." I take your panties from Lily's mouth. "Put these on and straighten your skirt," I say as I gently remove the nipple clamps.

"You have done well, Jenny. I'm pleased with you." The limo halts as you slide the top back on over your sensitive nipples. I step out of the car and pull you to your feet on the curb.

"You'll want to freshen up," I say, and you become aware of your smudged lipstick and disheveled hair. You are outside the main entrance to your office.

I kiss your forehead, whisper, "Have a nice day" in your ear, and get into the limo and leave.

PAGE TEN OF THE EMPLOYEE HANDBOOK

Alison Tyler

We should stop," you say in that semi-sweet, semi-smug tone of yours. "Really, we should." I can tell from the taunting look in your lovely large eyes exactly how you want me to respond. I don't need any additional hints, but you continue as if I do. "It's against the rules," you add, gazing down at the floor as if shocked by your own naughty behavior.

"What is?" I ask softly. "This?"

"Oh, yes," you tell me, playing coy now. "That's just wrong, wrong, wrong."

Now, I press you up against the wall of your office so that your palms are splayed flat on the wood-paneled wall. Then I slide that short black skirt up past your curvaceous hips. I take my time, because I like to admire the view. "Or this?" I whisper to you, my mouth against your neck, teeth poised and ready to bite. You can feel my hot breath on your skin, and that makes you tremble.

"That," you insist. "That's just flat-out unacceptable."

"Ah," I sigh. "This is all getting clearer to me. You're saying that I'm just not supposed to do this—" As I speak, I gently slip your lilac satin panties aside. I love these panties. The black lace trim is a total turn-on, and the way they perfectly and snugly fit your ass drives me wild. I know that you wore them for me, and that makes me even harder. The thought that you looked through all of the naughty knickers in your collection before choosing this particular set is an image that gives me pleasure.

Even though I do love occasionally absconding with your panties, slipping them into a jacket pocket to take home later and play with—this afternoon, I don't take them down. I just push the smooth, slippery fabric out of my way, and my finger-tips play an immediate melody over your clit. For a moment, I make you lose your cool. My fingers stroke and tap, and you suck in your breath at the first wave of pleasure.

You can't be so clever now, can you? Not as the shining wetness coats my fingers, as I push back up and stand next to you, staring directly at you as I lick your juices off the tips.

"Oh, God," you groan. You can't suppress the shudder that throbs through you as you watch. Don't you love the way that looks? Me slowly, so slowly, tonguing away your sweet nectar.

"Is *this* wrong?" I ask, reaching my hand up under your skirt again to collect a fresh dose of your honeyed juices on the tips of my fingers. The first taste of you has made me hungry for more.

"No, don't stop—"

At your request, my fingers probe deeper, and I hold onto you with one hand, keeping you steady as I finger-fuck that sweet pussy of yours. I want you to be ripe and ready for me by the time I take my cock out. You need all the lubrication you can get because I'm going to fuck you hard. Even harder than you're thinking about right now. I'm going to slam you up against the wall and make you forget how to be coy. How to tease me with those bedroom eyes of yours. Or should I call them "boardroom eyes"?

"I don't know," I say, dropping to my knees and bringing my face right up to your cunt. I breathe in, adoring the smell of your sex. The scent makes me dizzy with need. "If employees aren't supposed to date, then you probably shouldn't let me lick your pussy."

"Doesn't say anything about that—" you assure me in a rush.

"What do you mean?" I tease. "What are you implying? That we should sidestep the rules? That wouldn't be fair to the rest of the workforce, would it?"

"I'm just saying—" you start, but then you can't finish your thought, because my tongue is already tripping along the seam of your body, playing you so sweetly. I know how to take care of you. I know the little tricks that you like best. My tongue makes several smooth rotations right around your clit—not actually touching that hot little gem, just brushing around it carefully. Slowly. And then, right when you think you're going to die if I don't touch you where you want, I slide my tongue along your clit in one long brushstroke. You grip my hair and hold on, shivering, so close already that I'm sure you can imagine exactly how good it's going to feel when I let you come. But I'm not letting you. Not yet. With a slow and steady pace, I resume those lazy, crazy, everlasting circles that make you want to sprawl out on the plush-carpeted floor and let me just lick you for hours.

"So," I say, speaking right up against your most tender skin, "what would page ten have to say about this—"

"No, nothing, nothing," you whisper, and it sounds as if you're begging. You're the one who brought it up, though. Remember that when I make you bite down on your lip to stifle your screams of pleasure. You're the one who opened the manual and used a bright lemon-yellow highlighter pen to illuminate all the different rules we were breaking.

I can tell now that you're dangerously close, and so I stand up despite your whimper of protest, and I push against you. This is my favorite way to fuck, driving in from behind with both of us standing, but at first I simply let you feel my cock against you through my clothes. I want you to know precisely how excited I am. How ready I am for you. When you whimper again, I rip open my fly and pull out my rod. You're in the perfect position, back arched, poised to receive me. I wrap one hand around your mane of dark hair and tilt your head back so that I can watch your face as I slide inside you. That first deep push is unlike any other sensation. The way your body surrounds me is sublime.

God, are you lovely. Your eyes grow wider at the moment of penetration and then get a faraway look, as if you've just arrived at some wonderful distant location. That exotic location called "I've almost reached it." We both know all about that place. And I'm going to take you even farther—to a tropical island called "coming together."

Out in the hall, I can hear the bustle of secretaries working. Hear the voices and the sounds of their fingers on the keyboards. Their chitchat on the telephones. I hear the low, gruff talk as different employees hurry past the room. Everyone's busy. Everyone needs something. Nobody will bother us, though. That's not even a tiny worry on my radar screen. Officially, we're holding a meeting, the two of us—an important, private meeting—so we can take our time.

Our time to do all the things I need to do to you. And I need to do so many things. Rutting forward. Driving hard. I need to make you crazy with the fact that you can't make noise. You can't be loud.

I want you to be warm and pliant, relaxed and ready, for

what we're going to do next. Because this is what I think about it all, baby: If we're going to break those boundaries, we might as well do it right. Might as well really get down to business. Don't you agree?

TGIF

Saskia Walker

'd been counting off the days, and boy, had they ever dragged. But I figured that if I could get to the end of the first week, I could maybe make it to week two.

Maybe.

I just had to prove I could last through my one-month contract. Biting the bullet and taking an office job had been the absolute pits in the first place, but I couldn't drift from college course to college course any longer. The time had come to quell my rebellious streak, tame my multicolored mop, take out my nose ring and don an acceptably smart outfit. *What a crime,* I thought to myself, when I'd packed away my usual, much more alternative wardrobe, and headed for the temp agency.

The job I was assigned to was deadly. I was audio-typing debt-collection letters for a junior lawyer, and William had been junior forever. He stumbled into my office, blushing to the roots of his remaining few hairs, and deposited a stack of files and tapes on my desk. That was day one. Since day two, he'd left the stacks on my desk before I even got in, presumably in order not to have to make small talk with me, and then disappeared off to who knew where. Maybe he was expecting a simpering office mouse, not a frustrated rebel who responded sarcastically when he mentioned the pleasant weather we were having for the time of year.

Well, what did he expect?

The weather was outside the tinted windows and I was trapped inside. There was no decent company to chat with on breaks, and there wasn't even any eye candy in the vicinity. The building site opposite my nineteenth-story window was too far away to make out anything. That would have been something. All I got was a drifting tide of muck curtaining my window courtesy of the builder's activities, but no brawny guys to check out. Perhaps if I brought in a pair of binoculars I could get a better look, and if I got a better look, that might break up the monotony.

Mostly there was just me and Audrey in the offices. Audrey was the senior administrator and she sat reading magazines and filing her nails all day in the reception. She looked down her nose at me condescendingly whenever I came out of my cell for a coffee. The highlight of her work schedule seemed to be shuffling wannabe divorcées into the senior partner's office, giving appropriate murmurs of concern to their irate monologues about truant husbands. I wouldn't have been able to keep a straight face. Perhaps that's why I wasn't on the front desk.

Looking at the clock, I stood up. It was nearly midday, time for my third caffeine shot of the day. Thank God it was Friday. I was about to step out from behind my desk when darkness descended. I froze. A shadow had fallen across me from behind, from the window situated behind my desk. The shadow moved across the surface of the desk. My heart beat faster as I tried to make sense of it. Nothing had broken the light falling in the window all week. What could it be?

I turned and took in the sight that met my eyes. Standing in a suspended safety cradle was a window cleaner, moving a large squeegee over the surface of the glass with rhythmic agility, all the while watching me and grinning cheekily. He winked, obviously well aware he'd given me a fright. I managed to return his smile and waved at him, snatching up my cup from the desk to cover my awkwardness.

Something interesting had finally happened! And, *yes,* he was interesting. Ruggedly good looking, with several days' worth of stubble, tall, well-built, and bleached blond. He went about his work in a showy, nonchalant way that made it look a warm-up for dirty dancing. He moved his entire body, as if dancing to the music he was listening to via his headset, and rode his massive squeegee easily over the surface of the glass, his biceps flexing, his torso riding firm and strong beneath the T-shirt he was wearing. Sexy! My blood pumped quicker when I noticed he was eyeing me speculatively from head to toe. I leaned one hip up against the desk, toying with the mug in my hands, taking in the sight. Well, why not? He was doing the same.

When he'd finished his task, he dropped the squeegee, reached into his pocket, and pulled something out. It was a piece of paper. He scribbled on it with a stub of pencil, then held it up against the glass for me to read. I stepped closer and read the scrawled message:

GREAT LEGS. NEXT TIME WEAR A SHORTER SKIRT.

I smiled. I couldn't help it. He grinned, saluted, and hit a control panel, hanging easily on the ropes as the safety cradle disappeared from view.

Well, that had woken me up. Wear a shorter skirt? What a cad! Sure, I was up for some fun and games, especially with a

hunk like him, but when was the "next time" that he was referring to? There was only one way to find out.

"I just had the most amazing shock," I said to Audrey, as I
poured filter coffee into my mug. "Some guy was hanging on the
outside of the building cleaning the windows."

Audrey gave me a superior smile. "Not what you expect to
see this high up, is it?"

"Not exactly. How often do they come around? I'd like to be
prepared next time."

"Oh, usually every six weeks."

My heart sank. I'd be finished with my contract and gone by
the next time he appeared.

"Until they started the building work opposite," she added.
"It's every Friday on that side of the building now, so you'll have
to be prepared for another visit next week."

"Oh, I will be." I sidled off, trying to contain my smile.

That second week went much quicker. In fact, counting the
days off till Friday took on a whole new meaning. I was looking
forward to my visitor, instead of wishing the days away until the
end of my contract. I didn't even think of bringing the binoculars
in. I had something far more interesting to focus on: the arrival
of the dishy window cleaner. What would happen if I did as he
suggested and wore a shorter skirt? Where would it go then? I
raced through my stacks of audio-typing while at the back of my
mind I tried to decide what to wear.

Audrey commented on the fact that my typing had speeded
up. She had so little to do, she had to eavesdrop on me to fill
her timetable. If it weren't for the prospect of the window guy,
I would have told her to stick her job. She didn't approve of
me, that much was obvious from the start. I'd heard her on the
phone to the temp agency, asking if they had "anyone more
suitable, someone the right caliber to work in a legal office."

Too bad for her they didn't have anyone else, right? And she *so* did not approve when I arrived for work on that second Friday, wearing the leather miniskirt I usually saved for clubbing, knee-length boots, and a skin-tight lizard print shirt that dipped low into my cleavage. I waved when I passed her desk, where she sat open-mouthed, glaring at my outfit.

The morning went far too slowly, and I was up and pacing around between the desk and the window when the shadow of the cradle finally began to descend. This time I was even more mesmerized because, as the window cleaner lowered into my field of vision, I realized he was stripped to the waist. Boy, what a sight for sore eyes that was. He was built all right. All that physical labor had given him a great body, and the day was warm enough for him to sun himself while he worked. He grinned, eyeing me appreciatively as he washed the window. I reached for a piece of paper and wrote him a message:

GREAT ABS! DO YOU APPROVE OF THE SKIRT LENGTH?

When he broke into a laugh, I'd have paid highly to hear the sound of it. He nodded, his mouth forming a whistle while he eyed the gap between my boots and the skirt. With his eyes on me like that, I was suddenly aware of every inch of my body. My breasts felt tight. My sex was heavy, responsive to every signal he was giving me, to every nuance of his body language. I turned on my heel and gave him a better look, hands on hips. He reached into his pocket and scribbled on his notepad, slamming the paper against the glass:

OH, YEAH, THAT'S MUCH BETTER.

BUT I STILL CAN'T SEE WHAT COLOR YOUR UNDERWEAR IS.

I laughed. What a lad. Something about the setup, with him on the other side of the glass like that, made me feel even more daring than I might have under normal circumstances. I was no shrinking violet either way.

His squeegee was hanging idly in one hand; the other leaned up against the taut ropes of the safety cradle as he watched, riveted, while I slid one finger down into the front of my shirt, idly toying with the top button in my cleavage. He licked his lips. My sex clenched; my panties were already damp from expectation. Seeing him through the barrier of the impermeable glass had created a void of discovery, a safe zone to test each other out. I popped my top button, thrilled by the effect I was having on him. He mouthed something encouraging. I let another button pop open. He nodded, one hand gesturing for me to continue. I felt like I was part of an act in a live sex show. The thought spurred me on. I stepped closer to the glass. We were possibly twelve inches apart, but he was so untouchable. I undid the final two buttons, my hands pushing the fabric back to reveal my sheer lace bra.

He shook his head. His eyes glazed, and he ran one finger down the length of the glass in front of my breasts, smearing the damp glass with his touch. He continued to stare while he grappled in his pocket for his paper and pencil and wrote me another note:

WILL I GET TO SEE MORE OF YOU NEXT WEEK?

He scrunched the paper in his hand after I read it, and his eyes were molten with arousal. I nodded and blew him a kiss, winking. As he reached for the controls on his cradle, his other hand ran over the impressive bulge in his jeans, and he flickered his eyebrows at me. Then he was gone. Only the smear on the glass remained to remind me of what had passed between us, a sticky mark on the intervening sheer pane. I touched the inside of the glass, placing my own mark against his. Man, was he ever sexy. And he was making me so hot. I stalked over to the air conditioning panel and turned it up to full blast, my mind racing with ideas of how to up the ante the following week.

By the time that third Friday came around, I'd been thinking on it long and hard—I'd even dreamed about the guy twice. Both times it was the live sex show imagery, and the idea fascinated me. In the first dream, I was dancing for him, slow and sexy. He was riveted, sitting back in a low chair, his erection straining through his jeans. In the second dream, I stripped naked and then watched as he tried to lick my body through the glass. When I woke, I was twisted in my sheets, my fingers crushed between my legs as I wanked myself off.

My excitement level built over the week, and my imagination was running riot. To top it all, Audrey had pissed me off big time, which left me feeling even more rebellious. I was ready to pull pints in my local pub rather than listen to her miserable condescension a moment longer. That sense of rebellion and the fact that the guy had filled my thoughts all week long meant that I was edgy and high on my own physical arousal.

Thank God it's Friday, I murmured to myself yet again. But this time I smiled at the idea.

The window cleaner looked at my floating summer dress with a surprised expression when he winched down into view. I waved and then turned my chair to face the window, to face him. I sat down in it, staring straight at him, smiling. He wrote his message:

Hey, you're breaking my heart here.
That skirt is way too long.

He mimed an aching heart, his expression teasing me all the while. I shook my head at him, swinging my chair from side to side. Then I kicked back in the chair, one strappy, sandaled foot jamming up against the window frame, the dress sliding down my thighs and pooling in my groin.

Oh, yeah, he loved that.

I pivoted on one heel, my chair moving from side to side.

I knew he was watching the flash of the scarlet G-string I was wearing, and that fuelled my fire. Between my thighs, a nagging pulse begged for attention. I let my hand tease along the hemline of the dress. He lifted his head, his eyes on my fingers. I picked up the piece of paper I'd left handy and scribbled on it:

WHAT DO YOU THINK NOW?

Quickly, he replied:

I'D LIKE TO PUT MY HANDS UNDER IT AND TOUCH YOU.

It was just the kind of response that I'd hoped for. He was really up for this. I ran my hand over the surface of my G-string, one finger sliding beneath the fabric. He nodded his head, scribbling again.

YOU ARE SO BAD!

"You'd better believe it," I whispered, as I pushed my fingers into my damp slit, where my clit was begging for attention. With a quick, practiced action, I arrested it between two fingers, my whole body jolting with the sensations that instantaneously roared over me.

The guy started craning his neck, as if he could see inside my underwear if he tried hard enough. Logic had clearly gone from his mind by that point. For me, the fact that one gorgeous man was watching me, wanting me, completely mesmerized by what I was doing, was like a drug heightening the experience, channeling every dart of pleasure into a major roller-coaster ride. I slid down in the chair, my back arching against it as I worked my clit. My fingers were sticky, the flimsy fabric of my G-string quickly growing wet. His mouth was moving— he was saying something to himself, and his eyes were glazed with lust.

"Yes," I whispered at his silent form. "Yes." I managed to nod at him, my lips parting, when my clit throbbed unbearably and density gathered in my core. As I rode the wave, I became aware that he was moving. The cradle was disappearing from view. Had I gone too far? Had I embarrassed the poor guy? I doubted it—he'd pushed it along this far. And I'd really got off on the secret, silent performance for the man on the other side of the glass. My body was thrumming with sensation, my energy levels soaring.

I let my foot slide down from the window. I couldn't help thinking about how it might have looked to him, from the outside. Perhaps he'd gone off somewhere more discreet to have a wank. The idea infused me with a sense of raw power, heady and intoxicating. That was when I heard voices outside.

"Fuck." I tried to pull myself together.

There was some sort of disagreement going on in the corridor. Audrey sounded put out. I grappled my dress into place, spinning my chair to face front. The door sprang open.

"There must be some mistake," Audrey said, in a bewildered tone. "We had the interiors done just a few weeks ago."

"It's contracted, trust me."

I blinked, several times. It was him. He was there, standing in the doorway to my office. He'd put his T-shirt on, come inside, and found my office—and now he was walking in. Putting a bucket on the floor, he grinned at me and slammed the door shut behind him. A stifled cry of dismay came from the hallway.

Now what was I going to do? No glass shield, no gap the equivalent of thousands of square feet separating us. My blood roared, my heart thumping out a fierce rhythm. Given that I was already totally wired by what had gone before, his one-hundred-percent physical presence tripped switches I didn't even know I had.

"Sorry to interrupt, but I couldn't resist." He put his hands on his hips, observing me with hungry, watchful eyes. He was even sexier in the flesh, and the sound of his voice sent torrents of sensation over me. I was delirious with arousal, unable to stop myself responding in kind.

"Couldn't resist seeing it in the flesh, huh?"

He strode over. Pure testosterone oozed from him. Had I really caused this? Tut-tut, I mused—must be more circumspect around rampant males. I had to laugh. I couldn't believe he'd actually fought his way past Audrey and was standing right there in the office.

"You better believe it. That performance was enough to drive a man insane." He knelt down and swung my chair around so it faced him. His eyes were green, bright green. I ran a finger over his stubbled chin. He captured it in one strong hand, giving me a look that announced he was taking control of the situation now.

"I had to get me a closer look." The smile he gave me was full of raw, undiluted sex appeal.

Before I knew what was happening, he'd grabbed my legs and hauled them apart. If I thought my little bout of exhibitionist self-pleasuring had been hot, I wasn't prepared for what came next.

He ran his hands down the inside of my thighs, feeling his way toward the hot niche at their juncture. He stripped my soaked G-string down my legs, manhandling me with ease. The way he looked at me where I was wet from pleasure sent a hot wave of self-awareness over me. Then I suddenly forgot how to be self-aware when the tip of his tongue found its way into the sticky, cloying heat of my slit and he was eating me up. I nearly lifted off the chair!

His tongue was agile and intuitive. He explored the territory of my sex, before he began mouthing me, his tongue lapping against my swollen lips and over the jutting flesh of my clit. Rivers of sensation flew through my groin. My hands were knotting in his hair, my hips bucking against him. When he pushed an inquisitive finger inside me, I quickly came a second time, my body shuddering.

"Do you do this with every woman you meet courtesy of your squeegee?" I managed to ask, as I surfaced.

"Nope, most of them do a runner when I appear. Not you, though." He gave me that suggestive smile of his. He had one hand resting on his crotch, where he was rock hard inside his jeans. I was just contemplating how quickly I would hit the jackpot a third time if I had the pleasure of something that hard inside me, when I heard a sound.

"You're fired." It was Audrey. She stood in the doorway, her hands gripping the frame, glowering.

"Too late, I quit." Let's face it, it was only a matter of time before I walked out or got fired. It had been well worth it.

"I'm sorry," the guy whispered, one hand squeezing my thigh rather endearingly. He was genuinely concerned. What a sweetie.

"No problem, really. I was out of here anyway." I leaned forward and pushed my fingers into his hair, hauling his head back. I kissed his mouth deep and hard, reveling in the sense of deviance that roared in my veins.

I glanced over just as Audrey staggered backward in the doorway, shocked to the core by my response, her mouth opening and closing like a fish's.

The man kneeling between my legs followed my gaze and chuckled low. "If you're looking for a new job, we need a receptionist at HQ. It's not a posh place like this, but we have a laugh, and it does mean I'd get to see you again."

His smile sent an aftershock of pleasure right through me.

"Not to mention that a chick like you would be a hell of a lot more fun than the dragon they sent us from the agency."

"You reckon?" I asked, pushing him onto the floor on his back, straddling him and reaching for his belt.

"I reckon," he said, grinning widely when he felt my hand reach for his cock.

What is the old saying about being in the right place at the right time and grabbing opportunities when they come by? My hand tightened on his cock. It looked like office work wasn't going to be so bad after all.

AFTER HOURS

Marilyn Jaye Lewis

Whenever I'm out with Jack, I feel like I'm nothing but white trash. I revel in that feeling, though, and only he brings it out of me. He's known me too long and too well.

"Here, have a cigarette," he offers.

I take it, even though I no longer smoke. It's an unfiltered Camel, no less. "Jesus, are you trying to kill me, or what?" I lean my head closer to him and let him light the cigarette with his Zippo. I inhale. It's harsh and I feel like choking, but something about it is reminiscent of sex with him and I like it. I keep puffing on it and I get the feeling I'll probably smoke all night.

"Should we bring along a bottle of something?" he asks. "It would probably be polite."

"If you want to," I say. "But if we buy something too expensive, then I always end up wanting to hoard it just for us."

"Then let's pick up a bottle of something cheap for show and a fifth of something special to keep between ourselves."

"That sounds like a perfect idea. Make people think we're more generous than we really are."

When we arrive at the party, it's already in full swing. We know just about everybody there, and I'm getting a little bored with it—everything always being so predictably chic. What happened to those years when everything about going to parties seemed new and maybe even a little enticingly strange? Even when you did know everybody there?

"Remember when a Friday in New York was wildly exciting?" I ask him under my breath.

He looks at me and smiles wryly. "No. I can't remember back that far."

Jack and I are fuck buddies. We circle into each other's orbits when we're between significant others. Neither one of us is bold enough to take that step into marriage like almost everyone we know has already done—some of them, more than once. Beneath our respectable careers, our healthy incomes, and our trendy fashions, we're both still hopelessly immature when it comes to making serious commitments that involve the destinies of other people.

"Alison, hello there!"

It's my boss, Susan Krieger, the well-known architect, coming toward us. She's the female half of the very wealthy couple who's throwing this shindig. She looks astonishingly attractive. I always forget how good she's capable of looking when she's not seriously harried from too much work.

"Hi, Susan. You remember Jack? He used to work with us at the firm? In drafting?"

"Of course, Jack. How are you? So nice of you to come."

Susan is only slightly older than we are, but her fully loaded husband, Derek Krieger, has a good twenty-five years on most of us and more money than any of us can possibly imagine. He founded the Krieger Designs architectural firm in the late sixties and has been at the top of his game since most of us were still in college. He's not exactly handsome, but for a straight guy, he's always put an extraordinary amount of effort into maintaining his appearance. I guess he's what you'd call striking.

"God, she's a bitch," Jack says in my ear as Susan is walking away from us.

"She's okay. She's just one of those power gals."

"Who probably likes to be down on her knees when nobody's looking. Or getting stuffed in both ends at once by a couple of grease monkeys in some parking garage."

"Jesus, Jack." I give him an incredulous glance. "Where did that come from?"

"I don't know. Come on, let's go fill up some glasses and stash our booze somewhere safe."

We steer clear of the bar that's been set up for party guests in the living room and duck into the well-appointed kitchen, instead. We help ourselves to a couple of their good-quality drinking glasses. We press them under the ice dispenser in their oversized, stainless-steel refrigerator. The ice tumbles down into our waiting glasses with a crashing noise. At that moment, Derek Krieger comes into his own kitchen.

"Alison, Jack." He takes in the full scope of what we're doing with a stern expression. It's clear he hasn't forgotten Jack, his incorrigible ex-employee, in the slightest. "Feel free to help yourselves there."

He grabs a bottle of wine from the kitchen counter and leaves.

"I feel like we just got caught by the school principal or something. And we got a last-minute reprieve."

Jack chuckles. "Fuck him."

We fill our glasses with our own Ciroc and then stash the vodka deep in the Kriegers' freezer. We return to the party and act as if we were part of it. But we retain our own little world where we watch everyone else over the rims of our vodka glasses. We gossip between ourselves, we denigrate our friends, we mock the few party guests we don't know, and eventually we start to kiss discreetly and get horny. We go out onto the Kriegers' balcony overlooking Central Park and light up a couple of Camels.

"You want to leave?" Jack asks. "We could go over to my place and fuck like bunnies."

That sounds like an excellent idea. "Okay," I say. "Let's finish these and go."

Jack moves up close to me. "How long has it been since your pussy got good and fucked, Alison?"

"Too long," I answer quickly, practically chewing on the end of my cigarette. I follow each puff closely with a healthy gulp of vodka. Clearly, I'm craving something in my mouth. Why does he always get me so horny when we're in public?

"How would you feel about getting stuffed at both ends by a couple of grease monkeys?"

I smile at him over the rim of my glass. "You're such a sicko, Jack."

He smiles back at me, his coal-black eyes searing into me without flinching. "I still think about you an awful lot, Alison. The thought of you always comes to me when I'm jerking off, when I need a pretty girl in my head to get very agreeable."

"How agreeable do I get?"

"You do just about anything, honey."

I'm hot now. My panties are starting to get wet. The nicotine and vodka are buzzing cozily through my veins. I'm curious about my exploits. "So tell me some of the things you make me do?"

The balcony door opens and more smokers come out to join us.

"Hi, Alison."

"Hi, Tina. You remember Jack?"

"Of course I do. How've you been, Jack?"

I quickly put out my cigarette, hoping Jack will do the same so that we can leave. He does.

I want an answer to my question. I'm feeling seriously horny. "Tell me, Jack. I want to know."

"Let's go get another drink," he says.

I'm all for it, but I thought we were leaving. I follow him to the kitchen, anyway. Before we even refill our glasses, we're kissing. Slobbering all over each other. He pulls me up close to him. I hold onto his neck. His hands are under my skirt, up inside my panties, grabbing fistfuls of my ass while we kiss. He has a rock-hard erection pressing up against me.

When we break for air, I try again. "Tell me some of those things you make me do, Jack. I want to know how agreeable you think I am."

"Oh, just the usual," he says between kisses. "Mostly."

"What does that mean?"

"You know, you let me put my cock anywhere. Anywhere, anyplace, anytime I want it. You just come in very handy, that's all. Come on. Come with me."

"No," I protest on instinct, following him anyway. He leads me down the hall to the bedrooms and ducks inside one of them. "No, Jack, I'm serious. I'm not doing this in my boss's apartment."

"No one's going to know, Alison. Come on."

He pulls open a closet door. "Come on, come in here. Just a quickie until we get home."

I both hate and love this about him. He's irresistible when I'm horny. I follow him into the dark closet and we close the door.

In an instant he's tugging at my panties. "No, don't," I'm saying. "Keep them up. I don't want to be without my panties."

But he tugs them all the way down, clear down to my ankles.

"Step out of them, Alison," he insists in an urgent whisper. "Come on, take them all the way off."

For some reason, I do it. I guess he's right about my being so agreeable. It's dark, but he manages to extricate them from my high heels.

"Give them to me," I say.

"I'll just stick them in my pocket."

"No." But before I can protest further, he's pulled me up close to him again. His hands are up under my skirt, getting free rein of my naked ass.

I'm moaning deliriously into his kisses. As my eyes adjust to the darkness of the closet, I realize there are slats in the closet door, louvers, allowing air and some light to trickle in. I realize we'd better be extra quiet, though, because of those louvers.

"What are you doing?" I whisper suddenly.

"What do you think I'm doing, Alison? I'm going to fuck you."

"Jesus, are you serious?"

His cock is out and I can feel him trying to find my hole. He does. "God, you're wet," he whispers. "You little tramp."

I try to angle myself in a way that lets his cock get up me easily. I know I'm wet. I'm incredibly aroused. But this position isn't really working.

"Why don't you turn around?" he suggests quietly. "I'll try you from behind."

I turn around, leaning a little against the louvered door. His cock finds its way up my hole again. This position is definitely better. It feels incredible. I can't resist emitting a little moan.

Until the light in the room flashes on. Jesus. We are both instantly motionless, not making a sound. Someone is in the bedroom with us. No, it's two someones, and they're closing the door.

I can hear Jack quietly panicking in my ear. "Oh, shit," he says.

His cock is still nestled deep in my hole, his arms around my waist, holding me tight, but we don't move. "It's Krieger," he barely mouths in my ear.

Sure enough, Derek Krieger has come within view of the slats in the closet door.

Oh, shit, I'm thinking, not Derek. I'm feeling like he really is my school principal. That I'm in some serious trouble now.

Then a female comes into view. This is definitely not Susan Krieger.

Oh, my God, I'm thinking.

At the same moment, Jack mouths in my ear, "Christ, it's Veronica."

Veronica is Jack's ex-lover. Another architectural drafter at the firm. She's even younger than me. One of those lithe, help-less-seeming blondes from Connecticut.

"You're late," Derek is saying to her. He sounds angry.

"I couldn't get a cab…"

"Bullshit," Derek replies, cutting her off.

I'm stunned by his abrupt tone. What does he care if Veronica is late to his party? It's not as if any of us are on the clock. It's only a party, for Christ's sake.

Veronica is plaintive. "I'm sorry, Mr. Krieger."

Mr. Krieger? Nobody calls him Mr. Krieger—he's Derek.

"I absolutely couldn't help it. I couldn't get a cab."

"You should have thought ahead, young lady, and left earlier."

Derek's using quite an intimidating tone. Something here doesn't seem right. Then suddenly Jack's hand dips down furtively between my legs. His fingers deftly feel between my slick lips, looking for my clit. I can't believe he's trying to arouse

me now, here, with this going on. But I'm too nervous to pull
away, to make a sound. I'm still impaled on his cock.

In my ear, Jack says almost inaudibly, "I think he's going to
spank her."

I'm incredulous. "What?" I try to say.

"I know Veronica," he tries to explain. "Krieger's going to
spank her."

Well, I'm stunned again. But now I'm a lot more interested.
These two are having some twisted affair! I'm trying to get a
better view through the slats in the door without moving at all.
If Veronica is going to get spanked by Mr. Krieger, I definitely
want to see.

Jack's cock is reviving inside me, and his fingers have zeroed
in on my clit. I can't believe any of this is happening. I'm so glad
we decided to come to this party.

"I gave you specific instructions," Derek is going on.

"I know, but..."

"And I expected you to follow them."

"I know." Veronica is practically whining.

"I'm too busy to be wasting my breath on someone as incom-
petent as you are. You're over an hour late."

"I know, but I..."

"Save it, Veronica. Save it for someone who has time to give
a shit about your next lie."

"Oh, yes," Jack agrees quietly. "I know that feeling. I hope
she gets it good, the little liar—with her panties pulled down."

Her panties pulled down? That hadn't occurred to me.
I'm really on fire, overwhelmed by all the stimuli. But Jack's
commentary is making me feel too crazy. I don't want to get
caught here—I want the show to continue. I want to keep
watching.

"Come here, Veronica."

He's good, I'm thinking. Very stern. I'm actually a little scared for her.

He sits down on the edge of the bed. She moves only slightly.

"Right here," he says. "You can see where I'm pointing, can't you?"

"Yes."

"You're not having any trouble hearing me?"

"No."

That answer was barely audible. And Veronica doesn't seem to be moving.

"Derek," she pleads suddenly. "Don't make me do this. Your wife is practically in the next room. All those people."

"What did you call me?"

"I'm sorry—Mr. Krieger!"

Boy, he sounds menacing. Sitting on the edge of the bed like he is, I can easily see his face now and he looks deadly serious. I wonder if Veronica is really scared. She sounds it. I think I would be, too.

Jack is breathing heavily against the side of my neck, his cock working slowly inside me, methodically. He's soaking up every nuance of this scene, just like I am. I wonder how that must feel? Watching an ex-lover about to get disciplined? I wonder if they were into this spanking stuff when they were living together? Funny how much you don't suspect about people....

"Veronica, I'm waiting. The longer you put this off, the more you run the risk that my wife will come looking for me. Then how will we explain it? Not just to her but to a roomful of party guests?"

The sound of Derek's commanding voice is electrifying my clit, while Jack is giving it just the right pressure at the same time. This spanking stuff is amazing. I need to have a serious talk with

Jack about all this when we finally get out of this place.

A quick breath of lust is caught in Jack's throat. Immediately, I see what it is he's lusting over. Veronica's hands are up under her skirt. She's pulling her panties down. She's really doing it. She's moved in front of Mr. Krieger. We can see everything. With her skirt held high, Veronica lays herself across Mr. Krieger's lap.

I'm thinking, that's some ass she's got there, white and so perfectly round. I'm also thinking, I never once dreamed I'd see Veronica's ass—for any reason at all, let alone because of this.

Jack's cock is swelling up inside my cunt. He's giving it to me slow but very hard. I clutch at his arms, needing to hang onto something. The lust is galloping through me now. I want to cry out.

The spanking is swift and sound. Veronica tries hard not to emit even a tiny peep. I know she's afraid of being discovered. Maybe that's part of her thrill, who knows? But how she manages to endure those well-aimed, decisive smacks on her bare ass without once letting out a cry or a shout is beyond me. Mr. Krieger is not playing. His strokes are severe. Veronica's ass is already bright red.

I'm too enchanted to breathe. Jack's steady fingers have tripped the tremors of orgasm in me, and I have to endure the onslaught of pleasure in my clitoris without so much as making a move. He must know I'm coming. He's holding me very tight.

The spanking is over before I'm even through coming. Veronica is off Derek's lap, pulling her panties back in place. Derek is standing now, too. They kiss. They moan.

"Okay, kiddo," Derek says, giving her one last playful swat on the behind. "Let's get going."

They leave and suddenly the room is black again.

"My God," I say at last. "That was amazing."

Jack repositions himself to fuck me like crazy now. It feels so good, but it doesn't take long for him to come.

"Come on," he says, pulling out of me and zipping up. "Let's get out of here. Let's go back to my place."

"My panties, Jack. Give me my panties."

"I'll give them to you when we get home."

He lets himself out of the closet and all I can do is follow. It isn't the first time I've gone off with him without my panties. I just straighten my skirt and hope for the best.

We're down the hall in a flash. In the foyer, however, Jack remembers the Ciroc. It cost us nearly sixty bucks. "Go get the vodka," he says. "I'll wait here."

I dash back to the kitchen, oblivious to everything around me. All I want now is my vodka and to get to Jack's bed as quickly as humanly possible.

In the kitchen, I run smack into Derek, alone. I'm thoroughly startled and painfully conscious of not wearing any panties. I'm not quite sure how to explain why I'm taking an expensive bottle of vodka out of his freezer.

"I put it there," I try lamely, smiling at Derek. Now I see him differently. Now he makes me incredibly nervous.

He looks at me and says nothing.

"It's my vodka," I keep explaining, feeling sweaty between my legs. "I'm going now."

He just stands there, offering nothing. Silence. Just staring at me.

"Thanks for the party, Mr. Krieger." Jesus, why did I say that?

He raises an eyebrow. His eyes pierce me with the faintest hint of a questioning smile. "You're welcome, Alison. See you Monday."

MEMORANDUM

N.T. Morley

Notice of Disciplinary Action

To: Audrey Chivas, Executive Assistant
From: Tabitha Kelly, Office Manager
Date: 1 September
Re: Violation of Office Dress Code
Cc: All Staff

It has been brought to my attention, Miss Chivas, that you have violated our office dress code on numerous occasions since being hired by the firm on 10 August. When you accepted employment at our firm, you read and signed a copy of our office policies and procedures document, including our office dress code on page 14. Nonetheless, you have continued to violate our dress code.

I have listed the documented violations below; each was brought to my attention by a senior partner in the firm.

(1) On 11 August, your skirt was measured by Mr. Armando

Stern to be eight inches above the knee. On that day, you also wore pumps with four-inch heels, a clear violation of article 8 of our office dress code. A first-level warning was issued.

(2) On 12 August, your silk slacks were sufficiently snug that Mr. Stern was able to see your panty lines, and his comments on their visibility met with, by Mr. Stern's report (and as I witnessed first-hand), a careless dismissal of his concern. That is wholly unacceptable. Furthermore, on that day your leopard-print brassiere was quite visible through the tasteless lemon-yellow top you wore. Again, this behavior is unacceptable.

(3) On 15 August, your skirt was, as estimated by Mr. Spankett, six inches above the knee. Miss Chivas, I would like to point out that such a skirt is decent by perhaps four inches. I was out sick with bunions that day, but I have a reliable report from Mr. Stern, Miss Beck in Accounting, and George, our FedEx delivery person. In addition, Mr. Spankett was kind enough to provide a Polaroid he took that day, and I am appalled. I have enclosed said Polaroid here. Coupled with the four-inch heels you wore that day, not to mention the blatant display of what could only have been a push-up brassiere underneath your rather filmy blouse, this outfit presented a wholly unprofessional picture of our firm. A second-level warning was issued at this point.

(4) On 22 August, your dress was black in color, decent, again, by perhaps four inches, and was coupled with knee-high, lace-up boots with the Doc Martens tag clearly visible at the back of your calf. I admire your forward-facing fashion sense, as I admire your attempt to be accepted by the "in" crowd. But we are a place of business, Miss Chivas, not a Marilyn Manson concert.

(5) On 23 August, though your skirt was of acceptable length, your red lace panties were clearly visible underneath when you bent over during your rather ill-advised and lengthy session

of filing in the lower drawer in Mr. Grimm's office. Polaroid enclosed.

(6) On 25 August, you showed up to the office with your hair in pigtails, a white blouse thin enough to show your brassiere underneath, and a plaid skirt that came, again, eight inches above the knee. When asked to retrieve a file from the bottom drawer of Mr. Harshass's desk, you reportedly turned away from him, bent over fully without kneeling, and displayed your white panties to him most shamelessly. Again, Mr. Harshass thoughtfully provided a Polaroid, which I have enclosed. A third-level warning was issued, resulting in your being docked a day's pay, to which you responded with a shocking display of disregard for the disciplinary process, stating (and I quote): "Ah, motherfuck, I guess I'll have to make up the difference giving blow jobs down on the waterfront."

(7) On 26 August, when working a Saturday to help Mr. Stern prepare for a client meeting, you arrived at the office dressed in hot pants, a halter top, and platform clogs. Again, as reported by Mr. Stern (and demonstrated by the enclosed Polaroid), your panty lines were clearly visible under the shorts, though you didn't see fit to wear a bra under the halter top. I should perhaps clarify here that our office dress code is to be followed even when the position demands weekend work.

(8) On 28 August, you returned from taking your lunch hour in the company gym without changing out of your exercise clothes, shamelessly displaying the fact that you wore a white leotard that had become rather moist with sweat and therefore almost entirely transparent. A fourth-level warning was issued, resulting in this memorandum.

Miss Chivas, let me take this time to commend you for your excellent work on many other fronts. Your willingness to help out with client meetings has been quite admirable and has led to a number of important accounts being exceptionally well serviced by this office. The senior partners have repeatedly commented on your willingness to lend assistance in whatever way is needed. However, your interpretation of the company dress code clearly needs extensive correction, which I offer forthwith:

(1) As stated in our policies and procedures document, skirts for employees who measure five feet, three inches (as you do) are to be no less than eight inches above the knee; measured from the torso, hems are to remain decent by no more than two inches or (preferably) less. Heels on all shoes worn to the office will be no less than six inches, except on casual Friday, when five-inch heels are permitted.

(2) Silk slacks, as you well know, are to be worn without panties underneath (except on casual Friday, when a thong may be worn). Furthermore, you know quite well that employees with D-cup or smaller breasts (yours were measured to be a C cup) are not allowed to wear brassieres. On that day, this undergarment entirely disguised your nipples, which should have been erect and clearly visible throughout the day, as stated on page 16 of our office policies and procedures document. Also, animal-print clothing is strictly forbidden at this time. If the firm institutes a Trailer Trash Thursday, you'll certainly be the first to know. Last, when Mr. Stern offered his rebuke of your wearing panties with these slacks, proper office behavior and our specific policy required you to immediately remove the offending panties in front of him and feed them into the office shredder.

(3) Again, a skirt six inches above the knee is decent by perhaps four inches and therefore a full two inches longer than is permitted by our dress code. I must reiterate that heels are to be six inches, not one bit less. Last, when wearing a blouse as see-through as the one you wore that day, Miss Chivas, you should have known better than to wear a push-up bra. While I admire

your desire to display your breasts as attractively as possible, you know full well that such displays of your fetching knockers are required by our dress code to be much more blatant than is provided by a push-up bra. If you are in need of some support, Tamiko in the mailroom has volunteered to provide you with her particularly skilled version of breast bondage. Simply visit her on the third floor before you report to work.

(4) Our policy clearly states that black outer garments are unacceptable, as they overly camouflage what lies underneath. Furthermore, wearing flat-soled boots is well beyond the scope of acceptable dress at our firm.

(5) While red lace panties of the style you wore might, arguably, be allowed to slide on a casual Friday (given their little red hearts and bows on the sides), again, panties are expressly forbidden on all other days. Additionally, Mr. Stern found your shameless display entirely distracting, as he was attempting to spank his secretary Julia at the time.

(6) While your kinky little schoolgirl fantasy is commendable, I made it quite clear in your job interview that the only schoolgirl who belongs at Stern, Stern, Grimm, Spankett and Harshass is a *shameless slut* of a schoolgirl. While your skirt was quite attractive, it was entirely too decent for the office, and wearing a brassiere is unacceptable in all circumstances, regardless of how visible it is through your blouse. Furthermore, shamelessly displaying your white panties to Mr. Stern strikes me as another example of your willful disregard of our policies. As mentioned in earlier paragraphs, Miss Chivas, you should have been entirely nude under that pert little outfit of yours.

(6a) As a supplementary note to item 6, I should like to remind you that any income you derive from giving blow jobs down at the waterfront should be provided to me in cash (and preferably not in wadded-up little $1 bills) for laundering through the corporate account. We can't be too careful about those IRS sons of bitches, Audrey, now can we? They certainly don't appreciate the value of a good blow job the way our firm does.

(7) I should perhaps clarify here that our office dress code is to be followed even when the position demands weekend work. I applaud your adhering to our dress code by eschewing a brassiere under your halter (which would have been unflattering in any event), but you violated our dress code in two ways: first, by wearing panties under those skintight little hot pants (Did you get them at Next to Nothing? I've been thinking of picking up a pair of those myself) and, second, by failing to wear high-heeled shoes. Your platform clogs, while presenting an admittedly cute seventies trailer-trash image of your whorish little bitch self, Audrey, were again inappropriate for the office, even on a Saturday.

(8) As you know, the co-ed company gym is to be used only when fully nude. I should note that you looked adorable with your nipples poking out of that tiny little leotard thing, but please, in the future, remember to strip naked before mounting the stationary bicycles—and don't forget to wipe down your equipment afterward.

Audrey, please let me reiterate that your job duties on other fronts have been performed with great skill and enthusiasm. Mr. Stern frequently comments on the quality of your oral skills, and his secretary Julia particularly likes the way you always come when she spanks you. I myself have had the distinct pleasure of feeling you up on numerous occasions, and your juicy little cunt never fails to open right up to my mercilessly thrusting fingers. Furthermore, you look particularly eye-catching when you lift your skirt, drop to your knees and take it doggie-style; I think all of Stern, Stern, Grimm, Spankett & Harshass's partners will agree that you have the finest ass in town, and you never hesitate to give it up. Mr. Spankett, in particular, has commented that if you weren't a shameless little cocksucking whore, he'd love to take you home to mother.

But I must take this opportunity to ask you to reflect on whether full-time employment as a paid submissive in a private brothel for poontang-obsessed billionaires is truly your long-term career goal. While I admire your love of spankings and your unthinking devotion to taking it in those filthy little holes of yours whenever possible, not to mention providing orally for any rampaging hard-on that appears in front of you regardless of the identity of its owner, I question whether the willfulness and cheek you've shown in your tenure here isn't indicative of an unwillingness to wholeheartedly adopt a submissive posture. Perhaps you are what educated office managers call a "smart-ass masochist."

In that event, despite your disciplinary record, I question whether you wouldn't do better assuming a leadership role at Stern, Stern, Grimm, Spankett & Harshass. Julia and Tamiko have both expressed the desire to feel that firm hand of yours on their behinds—in Tamiko's words, to "see if that horny little cunt can give as good as she gets." I concur. Your impressive showing in the recent catfight with Antoinette over who would get the last Pixie Stick in the company snack room certainly displayed a propensity for uninvited dominance, and once you had the little slut in a headlock, you did show an estimable appreciation of the finer points of forced cunnilingus, not to mention great skill at the old "pile driver." Furthermore, your skilled applica-tion of your throbbing sex to the little bitch's mouth despite her crocodile tears really demonstrated an ability to turn any administrative situation to your advantage. The result was a full acceptance of her defeat by Antoinette; in fact, the girl saw me immediately afterward, and when I threw her over my lap for disciplining, I only had to spank her three times before the little vixen exploded in sobs of orgasm.

In short, you show a talent for exerting your own will, even in the face of resistant employees. I think you would make an excellent apprentice for me, Audrey.

Should you prove open to such an altered career path here at Stern, Stern, Grimm, Spankett & Harshass, I must caution you that along with the vastly increased salary and many career perks (frequent tongue jobs from your subordinates being not the least of them) comes a great deal of responsibility. It will require improved commitment on your part, not to mention an intense program of mentorship in which I will teach you a great deal about administering punishment to horny little sluts who think they know it all.

Audrey, I hope the choice is clear.

Please report to my office at 5:00 p.m. for further discussion of this matter.

Cordially,
Tabitha Kelly
Office Manager

RAT RACE

Nikki Magennis

No time, baby. We never have time. We get lost on the merry-go-round and caught in tangles of clocks, scissors, and telephones. Appointments stack up between us in prissy little numbers, stealing life by the hour. On the calendar we cross off days.

Rush hour. Traffic swarms around us. We suck in motorway fumes and listen to the ticking of the indicator. The radio blares. Horns bark. Slip your hand under my skirt, baby. In among the sweat and the heat and the underclothes there's pure, sweet desire. My wet cunt, the pulse that brings the world to a standstill.

ABOUT THE AUTHORS

XAVIER ACTON's writing has appeared in Gothic Net, Eros Zine, the *Sweet Life* series, the *Naughty Stories from A to Z* series, and many other anthologies. His weirdest job was editing web copy describing porn movies, which required documenting the sexual acts therein. It was weird. *Really* weird.

LISETTE ASHTON is a UK author who has published more than two dozen erotic novels and countless short stories. She writes principally for Virgin's Nexus imprint, as well as occasionally writing for the CP label Chimera Publishing. Her stories have been described by reviewers as "no-holds-barred naughtiness" and "good dirty fun." On the subject of her "oddest job," Lisette says, "On my official CV, the 'oddest' job included there is my time spent working as a funeral director's assistant. However, my philosophy about any job has always been if you get to stay indoors and they expect you to keep your clothes on, then it's not really hard work."

TULSA BROWN is a refugee from the prairies and from another genre of fiction. Her erotica has appeared in over a dozen anthologies, and she's twice been runner-up for the Rauxa Prize for erotic writing. She is the author of a gay romance novel, *Achilles' Other Heel* (available from www.torquerepress.com). Tulsa's character of Lise is her psychic twin.

RACHEL KRAMER BUSSEL (www.rachelkramerbussel.com) is a prolific erotica writer, editor, journalist, and blogger. She serves as senior editor at *Penthouse Variations,* hosts the In the Flesh Erotic Reading Series, and wrote the popular Lusty Lady column for *The Village Voice.* She's edited over twenty books of erotica, including *Rubber Sex, Yes, Sir, Yes, Ma'am, He's on Top, She's on Top, Crossdressing,* and, with Alison Tyler, *Caught Looking* and *Hide and Seek,* along with the nonfiction *Best Sex Writing 2008.* Her writing has been published in over a hundred anthologies, including *Best American Erotica 2004* and *2006, Everything You Know About Sex Is Wrong, Single State of the Union,* and *Desire: Women Write About Wanting,* as well as AVN, *Bust,* Cleansheets.com, *Cosmo UK, Diva,* Huffington Post, Mediabistro.com, Memoirville.com, *New York Post,* Oxygen.com, *Penthouse, Playgirl, Punk Planet, San Francisco Chronicle, Time Out New York,* and Zink. Her first novel, *Everything But...,* will be published by Bantam. In her spare time, she hunts down the country's best cupcakes and blogs about them at cupcakestakethecake.blogspot.com. Her oddest job to date involved begging for donations over the phone during college.

T.C. CALLIGARI lives on the West Coast in British Columbia, Canada. T.C. was once lured into being the payroll accountant for a guy who had a little shop and put cassette players into cars. At nineteen, she knew little about business practices but soon learned that the owner was dodging the bullet from a pack of creditors, and she was in their direct path. She didn't stay at the job for long. Previous erotica has been published in *Guilty Pleasures* and the Cleis Press books *B Is for Bondage* and *E Is for Exotic*. An erotic novel is also in the works.

JEREMY EDWARDS has been widely published online and appears in many print anthologies. His greatest goal in life is to be sexy and witty at the same moment—ideally in lighting that flatters his profile. His most unusual paycheck (to date) was earned by reading *The Decameron* into a tape recorder for a private client. Drop in on him unannounced (and thereby catch him in his underwear) at http://jerotic.blogspot.com.

JOLENE HUI is a writer-actress with a severe addiction to sugar. She's a horror buff who writes a column for TheFleshFarm.com. She also writes a column for InsideHockey.com. One of Tonto Books' first authors in 2006, she has also been published by a variety of newspapers, magazines, Cleis Press, Pretty Things Press, and Alyson Books. Her oddest job to date was dressing up as a saloon girl, speaking with an odd Old West accent, winking, and flirting while serving food. She still winks, but not for pay.

MAXIM JAKUBOWSKI has edited thirteen volumes of *The Mammoth Book of Erotica* and written six novels and two short-story collections in the erotic field. He is also active elsewhere and, by the time you read this, might even have completed novel number seven, *I Was Waiting for You*. Before he entered the literary (and erotic) galleys, he worked in the food industry and was, at some stage, responsible for all the orange soda drinks sold in the Congo and chocolate ice cream consumed in Finland. He lives in London.

SHELLY JANSEN is a bad girl in good-girl clothes. She writes text for medical brochures during the day and smut at night. Her most memorable job to date was iguana wrangler on a local production of *Night of the Iguana*. She was only late for work that one time.

MARILYN JAYE LEWIS's erotic short stories and novellas have appeared in numerous anthologies in the United States and Europe. Upcoming novels include *Twilight of the Immortal, Freak Parade,* and *We're Still All That*. Her oddest job was probably back in NYC in 1985, but she's not at liberty to really discuss it. She can only say it involved an Iranian and a briefcase with a lot of cash!

MIKE KIMERA was raised as an Irish Catholic living in England and now works as a management consultant living in Switzerland. At the age of forty-three, he started writing stories about sex and lust and the things they do to us, and seven years later he's still at it. As well as his book of short stories, *Writing Naked,* his work has been included in a dozen erotica anthologies. In 2005, he won the Rauxa Prize for erotic writing.

NIKKI MAGENNIS's work can be found in the *Wicked Words* anthologies (Black Lace), *E, F,* and *J* of Alison Tyler's *Erotic Alphabet* series (Cleis Press), *Yes, Sir,* from Rachel Kramer Bussel (Cleis Press), and *The Mammoth Book of Best New Erotica 7,* among others. Her first novel, *Circus Excite,* was published by Black Lace in 2006, and her next is due out in November 2008. She has been a gardener, barmaid, stage manager, civil servant, and life model. Her worst job ever was making pig swill in an army camp. Nikki lives in Scotland. Visit http://nikkimagennis.blogspot.com.

SOMMER MARSDEN leads her double life in Maryland. She's alternately a mild-mannered soccer mom and a dirty, dirty smut writer. Her oddest job to date was working as a framer at Ben Franklin. It only lasted one day, because every time she went into the basement where she was stationed, she passed out. Her work has appeared in numerous anthologies and online venues, including *Love at First Sting, Whip Me, Spank Me, Coming Together for the Cure, Ultimate Lesbian 08, I Is for Indecent, J Is for Jealousy,* and *L Is for Leather.* She is also the author of *Into the Light* and *Intruder.* More info can always be found at http://SmutGirl.blogspot.com as Sommer is a blogoholic.

N.T. MORLEY is the author of more than fifteen published novels of dominance and submission, including the *Castle* trilogy, the *Office* trilogy, and the *Library* trilogy, and is the editor of the double anthology *MASTER/slave.* Morley's strangest job to date was changing the sheets in a massage parlor that doubled as a dungeon.

CB POTTS is a full-time freelance writer, having neatly escaped the corporate world she writes about. She lives in the Adirondack Mountains of New York, balancing ghostwriting business books with penning sultry stories. Read about CB's latest goings-on at cbpotts.livejournal.com, including latest releases, upcoming events, and exactly what that strange noise from the garage turned out to be....

SAVANNAH STEPHENS SMITH is currently a secretary who harbors rather naughty thoughts as she types, files, and answers the phone from nine to five. She's the only one in her office who can make the printer behave, knows where the skeletons are, and how to change a ribbon on the typewriter...yes, the typewriter.

Her oddest job to date has been as a "belt mucker." Working underground at a lead-zinc mine for a few memorable summers, she was once assigned the task of "mucking out the belts." It was as fun as it sounds, but she was also licensed to operate diesel vehicles underground. Emerging into the light of day, she was also the "turn-down girl" at a rather swank hotel. Ever wonder who left those chocolates on your pillow? The turn-down girl, who drew the shades, pulled down the covers, and left something sweet in your bed....

The oddest thing **DONNA GEORGE STOREY** ever did for money was volunteer as a guinea pig for psych experiments in college. For the price of a dish of ice cream blended with Heath bars, she'd do things like read cards that put her in a self-loathing mood, look at pictures of random people and judge their attractiveness, then read cards that made her feel good about herself so she wouldn't commit suicide after the experiment. Her erotica has appeared in many cool anthologies like *E Is for Exotic, Naughty or Nice, Yes, Sir,* and *Dirty Girls,* and she's written a very dirty novel about Japan called *Amorous Woman.* Read more of her work at www.DonnaGeorgeStorey.com.

MARIE SUDAC's fiction has appeared in the *Naughty Stories from A to Z* series, the *Sweet Life* series, *Five Minute Erotica,* and many other anthologies. Her strangest job to date was either walking dogs—always an adventure—or maybe transcribing psychiatric reports, which was lots less fun but more memorable.

SASKIA WALKER (www.saskiawalker.co.uk) is a British author whose erotic fiction appears in over forty anthologies, including *Hide and Seek, Best Women's Erotica, Slave to Love, Secrets, The Mammoth Book of Best New Erotica, Stirring Up a Storm,* and *Kink*. Her erotic novels include *Along for the Ride, Double Dare,* and *Reckless.* Before becoming a full-time writer, Saskia worked in a diverse range of jobs, including being an extra in a historical romance movie. This job introduced her to the joys of wearing a corset, for which she is forever grateful.

KRISTINA WRIGHT is an award-winning author whose erotic fiction has appeared in over fifty print anthologies, including *Best Women's Erotica, The Mammoth Book of Best New Erotica* and *Dirty Girls: Erotica for Women.* She is also a college adjunct with a B.A. in English and an M.A. in Humanities. The most challenging skill she has ever had to master for a job was learning to keep a straight face when customers would pick up their candid sex photos at the one-hour photo lab she managed. For more information about Kristina, visit www.kristinawright.com.

ELIZABETH YOUNG has been many things, an art editor for a magazine, inventory manager at an art supply store, and a used-book buyer, but the one job she is most proud of is office manager at an escort agency, simply because it annoyed her mother so much. At this moment, Elizabeth can be found in Bethlehem, PA, living out her dream of being an under-employed freelance writer. You can read some of her work at www.antiaffirmations. blogspot.com; this would make her happy.

ABOUT THE EDITOR

Called a "literary siren" by *Good Vibrations,* Alison Tyler is naughty and she knows it. She is the author of a collection of short erotic fiction, *Exposed* (Cleis Press), and more than twenty-five explicit novels, including *Rumors, Tiffany Twisted,* and *With or Without You* (all published by Cheek), and the winner of "best kinky sex scene" as awarded by *Scarlet Magazine.* Her novels and short stories have been translated into Japanese, Dutch, German, Italian, Norwegian, Greek, and Spanish.

According to *Clean Sheets,* "Alison Tyler has introduced readers to some of the hottest contemporary erotica around." And she's done so through the editing of more than forty-five sexy anthologies, including the erotic alphabet series (*A Is for Amour, B Is for Bondage, C Is for Coeds, D Is for Dress-Up...*), all published by Cleis Press, as well as the *Naughty Stories from A to Z* series, the *Down & Dirty* series, *Naked Erotica,* and *Juicy Erotica* (all from Pretty Things Press). Please drop by www.prettythingspress.com.

Ms. Tyler is loyal to coffee (black), lipstick (red), and tequila (straight). She has tattoos but no piercings, a wicked tongue but a quick smile, and bittersweet memories but no regrets. She believes it won't rain if she doesn't bring an umbrella, prefers hot and dry to cold and wet, and loves to spout her favorite motto: "You can sleep when you're dead." She chooses Led Zeppelin over the Beatles, the Cure over NIN, and the Stones over everyone—yet although she appreciates good rock, she has a pitiful weakness for eighties hair bands. In all things important, she remains faithful to her partner of more than a decade, but she still can't settle on one perfume.

Visit www.alisontyler.com for more luscious revelations or myspace.com/alisontyler if you'd like to be her friend.